THE GIRL THAT *Chased* WILD HORSES

DWS WALTERS

Copyright © 2025 DWS Walters.

All rights reserved. No part of this book may be reproduced, stored, or transmitted by any means—whether auditory, graphic, mechanical, or electronic—without written permission of both publisher and author, except in the case of brief excerpts used in critical articles and reviews. Unauthorized reproduction of any part of this work is illegal and is punishable by law.

ISBN: 979-8-89419-680-0 (sc)
ISBN: 979-8-89419-681-7 (hc)
ISBN: 979-8-89419-682-4 (e)

Because of the dynamic nature of the Internet, any web addresses or links contained in this book may have changed since publication and may no longer be valid. The views expressed in this work are solely those of the author and do not necessarily reflect the views of the publisher, and the publisher hereby disclaims any responsibility for them.

One Galleria Blvd., Suite 1900, Metairie, LA 70001
(504) 702-6708

CHAPTER One

Her name was Samantha she was a young girl that liked to spend the warm spring afternoons down by the little creek hanging around the big cottonwoods and laying in the soft warm grass. There was just something about the sounds of the water making it's way over the rocks and the wind coming through the tall grass under the giant cottonwoods that made her feel at peace. She could come here to be alone or to day dream about so many things, sometimes she would bring her big drawing tablet and work at drawing the big trees and the birds and small animals that were always around them. Sometimes she would bring a book and just set in the sun and read. It was her special place. She had discovered this place one day while she was taking a walk, she was walking down an old cow trail being lost in her thoughts she had walked further than she usually did, when she realized that she was in an unfamiliar area she stopped and took stock of where she was. At first all she could see was the tops of the big trees, seeing how she had already come this far she thought to herself she just as well check it out since she was so close. As she walked toward the trees she soon realized that there was a deep creek bottom that she was not able to see from her house. She kept walking on the old cow trail and it lead her down into the bottom where the little stream was running. Once among the big trees she had to just stand there in awe of the great trees. The little stream winding it's way down through the middle of them and the tall grass reaching across the entire bottom which was maybe two hundred yards wide at this place. Unfortunately it was already getting late when she got there so she could only stay for a few minutes but she was sure she would be back soon, real soon.

As she was hurrying home she was excited about her new discovery. It seemed that since her family had moved to this place there was nothing but new and exciting discovery's. It was a big change for the paved streets and concrete side walks the she had learned to ride her bike on when she was so small. Her mother had inherited this place it had been an old cow camp way back when the big ranch at the head of the valley was in it's hay day. After the founder and patriarch passed away suddenly the estate had, had to sell off some of the more distant properties in order to satisfy the inheritance taxes. Her mother's uncle was a long time and valued employee of the ranch and he had bought this camp and four sections of pasture land to go with it long ago. There was the big two story house that they lived in, inside of it hung many pictures and paintings of western scenes along side of them were many photographs of horses and men. A big horse and hay barn, that was also a great place to play, inside the barn was a large tack room filled with saddles and bridles many of the bits silver mounted, the saddles all hand made by well known saddle makers of the time. Several of the saddles had been on many horses, had gone lots of miles and had seen hard use. There were deep grooves in the horns that had been burned into them by ropes dallying around and sliding slack. The seats were worn smooth, thin, and shiny, there was rawhide reins hanging on pegs along with multi colored hair ropes and rawhide bosals. The tack room was a place were time had stood still there were countless untold stories setting and hanging in there, it was like a small museum. Two sheds, a little shop, the little shop was neat and well organized all the tools were in there place and there was place for everything, and there was a little building that her dad had turned into a house for their little herd of chickens. There was a sturdy set of pole corrals, a good round pen and two bigger corrals coming off of the lean to on the side of the big barn. Over by the two smaller sheds were some smaller pens that had been used for cows, a horse trap and two smaller holding pastures that were called the Night traps. The rest of the four sections had never been fenced it had remained open range with the surrounding country. After the big ranch sold the camp and four sections the man running it at the time had made a long term agreement with her mother's uncle to lease the remainder of the four sections back and they would continue to graze it. It had worked out well for the uncle they had paid him good money for the lease and it had never been fenced. The ranch even made an agreement to maintain the barns and corrals so they could use them when needed. Little changed with the sell of the land and the buildings. It had been a good deal for the uncle, it had given him security and a place to call his own. It had been a great place for her mother to come in the summer times and great place for a young girl to learn about horses and how to ride.

Her mother had been the only child out of her brothers and all of her cousins that had ever showed any kind of interest toward her uncle. Her and her uncle had a lot in common she had always liked horses and he always had quite a few around, she would come in the summer time and she would go with him horseback and they would cook up all kinds of things. It had been a special and important part of her growing up many of the things the her uncle had taught her about horses were still part of her everyday life. He had been a very savvy horseman and he had been generous in teaching and sharing with her, when he passed he had left her everything. When she had been in college she had spent two summers working for a cutting horse trainer there she had been able to put into practice and have a better understanding of many of the things that she had learned from her uncle. There had been a lot of Aw-Haw moments. Here she loped horses for the trainer and she along with another young fellow rode colts every afternoon after the horses in training were worked. By being able to get on and ride so many horses under the supervision of the trainers and the other people that worked there she had been able to polish her skills as a horse person. After she finished school she had become an accountant later becoming a CPA and had worked in a big accounting firm when they had lived in the city. When she finished school she was recruited by the firm and went straight to work for them, after that it became harder and harder for her to find time to come and visit her uncle something that she looked forward to and longed to do. Her work seemed to take her further and further away from the things that were so close to her. Her mother had been the main supporter of the family when her dad had went back to college to finish his degree. Her dad was from a rural farming community and had gotten an Ag Engineering degree.

When her mother's uncle had passed her dad had just finished his degree, her mother wanted to come to this place right away but her dad wasn't so sure until he found out that they were needing an extension agent in the local community. When he went in to inquire about it he was almost hired on the spot. So the decision was to leave the city and move to the place that her mother's uncle had left was an easy one to make. Her mother had opened a small office in the little town and for about four and a half to five months every year she would do peoples taxes. During that time it seemed like they hardly got to see her, she would leave early in the morning and get home late every night, then it was over. That left her the rest of the year to work in her yard and have a nice garden. Her dad stayed very busy helping the local farmers and ranchers with projects that helped improve both their livelihood and their properties. He said it was satisfying work.

They had been here for a little over two years now she had not been very big when they first moved in her mother had wanted to get a couple of horses that they could ride but her dad had nixed that idea for the time being anyway, but she was pretty sure that her mother would win out on this idea, the time just wasn't right yet. At the start Samantha wasn't able to go very far out side of the building and corrals, but as she got older and became familiar with more things she was able to go further and further until like the day she discovered the big cottonwoods and the little creek bottom. That had been her best discovery that was her special place. She had become a good student of nature and had become very observant of the things around her, she was comfortable being alone in the big open spaces. She had come to really treasure this side of the valley with it's grass covered floor at the foot of the mountains that seemed to just rise up out of the valley. She had always wanted to go into those mountains and she was sure that someday she would.

It had been one of those first warm days of spring the sun was bright and there was not a breath of wind, the birds were happy with the way the day turned out as well they were singing and calling out to each other everywhere.

CHAPTER
Two

They had come down into her valley looking for food and water when they were forced out of the mountains by the harsh winter weather the wind and snow pushing them further down into the valley. This was the case when the girl first discovered the little band of horses that had seemed to appeared from out of nowhere and were grazing on the far side of the valley. Even though the winter had been extremely cold and bitter, especially on the mountain, there had been very little snow and what little snow fell had, had little to no moisture. It had only made what little grass was left harder to get to and so the horses had become more and more weak and thin as the winter had drawn on. It was on a bitter cold, and windy winter day that it seemed one of the older mares head came up as if she had remembered something from long ago. The other horses though cold and weak sensed something with the mare and they began to look as well. When the old mare moved off the other horses followed her as she began working her way down and across the snow covered slope. She took her time and went slowly over the icy slopes steadily making her way around, over, or through the wind packed snowdrifts, working their way into the lower slopes and over the divides until the snow was not as deep and the slopes were not so icy. By the end of the day she had led them into some lower country where the snow was not as deep and there was some grass to be found around the trees and brush. It was better here and the wind was not as strong and bitter as it had been on the higher ridges. After a short time of grazing the mare seemed to still not be satisfied of her new location, soon she was moving again. The little bit of grass and the nicer temperature had only seemed to reassured her that she was going in the right direction. As she moved out again the other horses followed her. This time her direction was more direct and her pace had increased considerably.

As dawn broke on the fifth day the small band of horses moved out onto the valley floor, they had left the cold and angry mountain far behind. The grass was tall and untouched with a small stream running with clear, cold water not to far from the ridge. Even though the horses were tired and weak from the long trek across and down the mountain they were hungry more. The horses dropped their heads and began to graze, they grazed until the sun had made it's way up into the sky and across the valley floor. With some nourishment in their bellies and warmed by the sun the horses began to rest. Soon the horses were standing heads down dosing in the sun, as the sun warmed them they all let themselves go, flopping down to lay stretched out flat on the ground.

It was here that Samantha first discovered the horses, at first she thought that she had gone crazy and her mind was playing tricks on her. As she moved closer she realized that there was indeed a small band of horses dosing in the sun near the edge of the stream in the dry deep leaves from the huge old cottonwoods that carpeted the ground next to the stream and under the trees. They were sleeping soundly as if they hadn't had any sleep for quite a while, she was very careful not to disturb them. Where had they come from? Who did they belong to? As she got closer she could tell that they had traveled far and that they were in pretty bad shape. Their hair was long and their manes and tails were long and matted, looking closer she could see that their ribs and hip bones were sticking out. Not only were these horses tired they were hungry, very hungry. The girl was able to get fairly close on this first encounter, the horses had been put into a deep sleep with food in their bellies and being warm from the sun for the first time in weeks they had gone into a deep slumber. The girl crept as close as she dared without disturbing them, from her place of hiding she watched with a curious fascination that she had not felt before.

The sun was warm, it was one of the last days of winter and it was a perfect day to lay in the warm deep grass and watch these creatures new to her valley. Soon she to had fallen asleep and for how long she slept she did not know, but when she awoke the horses were starting to stir. There were a couple of the ones that were laying down made a couple of half-hearted attempts at a roll, mainly just rubbing their head on the ground and rocking their body a little then they raised up on their bellies nose on the ground then set up and from there they rose to their feet giving a little shake. The dust kind of made a little cloud as it drifted from their sides and backs. One by one they walked over to the stream took a long drink of the cold water, then they were back with their heads down grazing in the tall grass.

The girl continued to watch from her hiding place, There were seven horse total their hair was so long it was really hard to tell just what color they were, but it looked like there were two brown ones, two were bays, one sorrel, and two were of a color that she had never seen before. Their mains and tails were black but one the coat was a reddish color with white hair mixed in and the other was more black almost a blue color. She had never seen these two colors of horses before she was very curious about these two, maybe she would have to ask the man at the end of the road about them he seemed to know a lot about horses. Of the two brown colored horses one had a white spot in the middle of it's forehead with white below the ankle on the left hind foot. The other one only had a small white snip on the nose that went down to the lip there was no other white on this one. One of the bays had a white streak that was the length of the face with two white feet in the back and one front foot on the left. The other was a solid bay and seemed to be the leader. The sorrel had a streaked face with one white foot on the left hind. The two odd colored horses neither had any white on the face and the reddish one had a white left hind. The more blue almost black looking one had a white front foot and a white hind foot both on the left side.

The sun was starting to sink and the shadows were starting to get long as Samantha watched from her place of hiding. She watched as the horses continued to graze, luckily they had chose to graze in the opposite direction from her. She watched and when she thought that she would not be seen by them she started working her way out of there. By taking much care and caution and by using the tall grass she was able to work her way back to the grassy draw that ran toward her house. Once in the safety of the draw she was able to stand up and walk again. She did not see the bay mare raise her head and put her nose into the breeze and take a big sniff, looking over her back in the direction that the girl had gone.

The walk back to her house didn't seem to take long at all, she was so caught up in her thoughts and her new discovery. She was so excited about her day that her evening chores were only a blur, it wasn't until she sat down at the table for supper that she even realized that she was so hungry. She had been so busy watching the horses that she had forgot all about food. As excited as she was about finding the horses, now she was not sure if it was a good idea to tell anyone about her discovery, just yet anyway. She didn't want any harm to come to the horses by the looks of them they had, had a hard enough time already. They sure didn't need anymore.

After Samantha had finished helping her mother clean off the table and do the dishes she went up to her room. She was concerned with the thought of the horses, it had not occurred to her until she was back home with her family that others might not be as excited to see the horses as she was. She had heard stories of when the valley was full of horses such as these. Most of them had been captured and sold or made into productive using horses for the area ranches. Some had gotten away into the harsh but safe arms of the mountains. Could these horses be what was left from the horses that had escaped into mountains years ago? Or could they just be some ranch horses that had been turned out for the winter and wondered off winding up here in the valley? She had only heard the stories this had all happened before her family came to the valley. So many questions and so few answers. Clearly she was going to have to pay the man at the end of the road a visit to find out more about what had really happened.

Samantha's head was spinning with questions and the events from the day, when she finally got into her bed, it seemed like forever before she finally dropped off to sleep. Her dreams were of tall grass and horses grazing, it was peaceful in those dreams. She woke up early when she heard her mother making breakfast. She was a little puzzled about her dreams thinking maybe she just dreamed the whole deal about the horses being in the valley. As the fog from her sleep slowly moved out of her head she remembered that it was not a dream and that the horses really did exist. After washing up and brushing her teeth and her hair she sat down at the table realizing that none of the answers to her questions had come to her in her sleep.

Since it was a school day the girl did not have time to make the trip down the valley to check on the wild horses. The days were still pretty short and after school and after finishing her chores at home there was just not enough daylight left in the day to make the trip. Her day had been busy with things at school, but not so busy that her thoughts kept going back to the horses. She was now more curious that ever about these horses. Why wasn't there any young or little ones? Surely some them were females. So many questions. She was going to have to make the trip again just as soon as she could work out a time, she also wanted to go talk to the man that lived at the end of the road. She was sure that she could find out more about the past that these horses came from. If not him he would know someone that did know. The afternoons were still just to short for very much other than chores and school work.

Everyday was pretty much the same do the morning chores go to school, come home do the evening chores have do the school work clean up the supper dishes take a shower then go to bed. Since the weather had been nice she had not been really concerned about the welfare of the horses, obviously the were in a much better place than where they had came from. She was just going to have to wait until the weekend to go and check on them again. The good thing was that had plenty to do and that helped keep her mind from drifting back to the horses….. most of the time anyway. They were never very far from her thoughts either awake or asleep.

Finally the weekend arrived and there had been no schoolwork to be brought home to do over the weekend. Samantha was excited as she finished her chores and set the table for supper, she was already making her plans for tomorrow as she finished doing the dishes. Getting into bed that night she had the same feeling as when she was a very small girl waiting for Santa. That was the kind of excitement that she finally feel asleep with. The girl was awake early and was out of bed as the dawn was making so that you could see outside. Her mother was already in the kitchen working on making breakfast for the family. She could smell the fresh coffee brewing and the smell of fresh cooked bacon drew her in like a moth to a flame. She knew her mother would be making fresh biscuits to go with all of this along with some fried eggs. Maybe even some gravy. She walked into the kitchen as her mother was dipping the biscuits in the fresh bacon grease as she was placing them into the frying pan to go into the oven. Maybe there was still some honey left from last season. That would be perfect!

As soon as the breakfast dishes had been done she was out the door doing her morning chores, as the last one was finished she looked down the valley toward where she had last seen the horses. She wondered if they would still be in the area that she had last seen them. Soon she was on her way heading for the big grassy draw that would get her close to the area that she had last seen the horses. The sun was well into its morning routine as she made her way it felt warm on he shoulder as she kept her pace. Unlike when she had left the horses the trek down the draw seemed to take forever. When she finally arrived at the place where she had first seen the horses she began to feel herself shake a little from the anticipation of seeing the horses again. She was a little disappointed when she crawled over the rise and there were no horses to be seen. Disappointed but not surprised, after all they did have four legs and they moved around a lot. As she walked over to where she had last seen them she noticed that there was a lot of manure piles all around and the grass was considerable shorter in this area. There were several places where she could tell that they had laid down for long periods of time and when she came across a bare sandy spot she could tell they had made good use of it, pawing and rolling many times. As she walked around looking at all of the sign that they had left behind she thought about the mystery novels that she like to read. This was like a crime seen and she was the detective looking for clues and putting together what all had happened here for the last week.

After spending the better part of an hour looking for "clues" she widened her search and slowly figured out the direction the horses had went. She knew that they would not be very far from the water she began to work her way down the stream, all the while looking for signs that the horse might have left. As she worked her way down country she began to notice that the sign was becoming fresher as she went, this was a good sign that she was at least going in the right direction.

When she finally came upon them it was more of a surprise than what she was expecting. She had been so busy looking for clues and she had forgot to look up. As it was she started over a little knoll when boom there they were right at the bottom in a little grassy bowl not more than thirty yards away. She automatically dropped to her stomach, she was so excited and scared that she had been seen and that they would run off that she forgot to breath for a minute or so. Luckily they were in the same condition as when she saw them the first time. The warm morning sun had worked it's charm on the little band of horses again they were dosing in the sun heads down some even laying flat on the ground. When she finally quit shaking and began to breath again she was able to let out a small sign of relief. She had not disturbed them and she had not been noticed. As she lay there in the tall grass she was able to observe that the horses did look much better that when she had seen them a week ago. Their flanks were fuller and not as gaunt, their hair was still long and their manes and tails were still kind of matted. It would only be a matter of time before they would shed their long coats of winter for the shiny coats of summer. That would come with the warmer weather and greener grass.

For what seemed hours she lay there watching the little band of horses. The ones left standing their heads would slowly sink lower and lower then one by one they would just flop down stretch out and go into a deep sleep. Only a couple remained standing. As they lay the there were small dust clouds coming from the dust beneath their nostrils, she was pretty sure that she could even hear some of them snoring. They were down for the count.

When they finally began to wake up and move around it was much like before. Some of them kind of rubbed their heads on the ground and groaning before setting up then rising to their feet and shaking off, some of them giving a big stretch before moving off to the stream to get a nice drink of cool water. They drank deep and she cold see their throats move with every swallow that they took. When they had drank their fill of the cool water they began to graze again, heads down and grazing away. The girl started thinking about making her move to leave without being noticed. She had to lay still waiting for the small band of horses to graze far enough away the she could make her move, it seemed like it took a long time for them to move very far at all. Finally they grazed their way over a little rise just enough that she could no longer see their heads. That was when she made her move, she turned around and crawled as fast as she could down the knoll until she was certain that she was completely out of sight. She then made her way back to the big grassy draw and started her long walk back home. When she had the opportunity to look back to see if the little band of horses had seen she could see that they were still heads down grazing undisturbed.

The walk home was longer than she remembered it to be and it was later than she had planned to be making her return trip home. She was going to have to step out pretty good in order to get back in time to finish her chores before dark. That was ok it was nice early spring afternoon and the sun was still warm on her face and she had laid still for so long that she had gotten a little stiff, so it felt good to be walking at a faster pace than she normally would have. There were a lot of things that she wanted to know about this little band of horses. Maybe tomorrow she would make the trip to go see the man at the end of the road and see if he could help answer some of her questions. Yes that would be the plan.

CHAPTER
Three

Samantha was up early again her mother once again was already up making another great breakfast. After the clean up from the breakfast and the morning chores were done she went to the shed and got her bicycle and headed up the road, she was going to see the man at the end of the road. She peddled and peddled she did not remember it being so far to this place. She had only been here one time with her father when she was just a small girl. She had never forgotten that trip or that place. There was a big barn with lots of big trees all around it and there was a large set of corrals that were made from poles and they were all very high. Not like most of the pens were they worked cattle down in the valley. Tucked back in the corner under some more trees was a neat little house with a small yard and there were places all around to tie horses up. That was all that she remembered. She sure didn't remember it being so far up the road. The good thing was it would be down hill on the way back.

As she peddled her bike into the compound there was sweat rolling down her cheek the sun had been warm and the continuous incline had been a good work out for her. She looked around as let her bike roll to a stop, it was much like she remembered except there were a couple of more houses and more out buildings than she remembered. The compound was located at the very head of the valley less than a half a mile above the compound the terrain made a very abrupt change into a slope that looked like a V shaped funnel that came form two sides into the compound. The two ridges that acted as the borders to the valley came together at the point of this V making everything livestock and water drain right through the center of the compound. Whoever had first picked this spot had given everything a lot of consideration. Everything was in the right place.

As she looked around she saw the man turning a horse loose into one of the high pole pens, as he finished closing the gate he looked up and saw the girl stand by her bike. He hung the halter on a hook near the gate and started walking toward the girl. As the man approached the girl took in everything about him, he was tall and slender built, his legs were bowed, he walked with smooth stride that had a quiet energy to it that she had never noticed in a person before. It was like he was not hardly moving yet he was moving smooth and quickly. The girl could still feel a little trickle of sweat come down her cheek as the man stopped in front of her. He kind of smiled then he said "you should get you a horse it's a lot less work". The girl introduced herself then she blurted out "can you tell me about the wild horses"? The man gave her long and steady gaze that seemed to last for a long time, he said "nice to meet you Samantha my name is Keith" then he invited her over to the shade of a nearby tree. Near the tree was a trough with water free flowing from a small pipe through it, there was a post with a dipper hanging from a nail, he offered her a drink of water which she gladly accepted. The bike ride had made her very thirsty. The water was sweet and cold it felt good going down.

As she looked around she noticed that there were four tree stumps setting in a circle they had been cut to a length that was just right for sitting, this was clearly the spot where many discussions had been had, many deals had gone down and many dissensions had been made right under this old tree next to the trough with the free flowing water. The man offered her a stump she sat down looking around not really sure what she was looking for or what she expected to get from all of this. That is when the man ask her "what would you like to know about these so called wild horses"? That is when she told him about her finding the little band of wild horses down in the valley. The man sat there very quite listening to everything that she told him that she had seen. She did not know why but she never gave it any consideration whether or not the man could be trusted knowing about the little band of horses. Maybe she just needed to tell someone and he was the closest she could find that might feel the same a she did. Either way it felt good to finally tell someone about the horses. The man was quite intent on listening and when she finished he sat there for several moments deep in his own thoughts. There was a brief moment where the girl had a bit of a panic when she thought what if he wants to go capture or even shoot the horses as she had heard had happened to some in the past.

When Keith finally spoke it was soft he ask her if she could describe to him what these horses looked like? That is when Samantha told him about the colors they were and how skinny they had been. The man shook his head as she was describing to him about the colors and when she told him about the two that were colors that she had never seen before his eyebrows went up and slight smile went across his lips. He seemed amused by what she had told him, then he told her that the colors were called "roan" one was a bay roan and the darker more blue was a blue roan. He then went on to tell her that there had been a red roan stallion that had belonged to a man that had a place across the mountain to the east most of his country ran out onto the big flats that were on that side, his headquarters was next to the rim rocks on the lower end. He also said that this particular horse the color was sometimes referred to as a "Strawberry roan" the old stallion had turned up missing for a while several years ago the horse was pretty old at the time and he had a bad knee from a severe kick several years before. When they finally found the old horse he was running with three mares two browns and a bay, the bay appeared to be the leader. When the ranch hand found them he was not really prepared for what he found he was riding a motorbike. He was pretty sure that he could gather and bring all of the fillies in with the old roan stallion, but he highly underestimated the speed, endurance and determination that these horses possessed. He wound up crashing the motorbike breaking some ribs and his collarbone in the process, having a long, painful walk back to the ranch. When he went after them, the three mares were young and very fast they went straight for the mountains like they had done it before leaving the old horse far behind. The three mares had never been seen in that country again. One of the cowboys came back and caught the old roan stallion and led him back to the ranch. The old roan stallion had died a year or so later. These would have been the last set of colts that he sired. The old roan had been the last stallion that had been on that side of the mountain as far as the man could remember. He said "more than likely the two roan horses had been sired by this old roan stallion. This should have been a really nice crop of colts the roan horse had been well bred and had produced a lot of good horses for that man. Apparently the two colts born the following spring had both been filly colts, and that would explain why there had not been anymore offspring from this group of horses they were all female or mares. But what about the sorrel and the bay with all of the white on it? Where did these two come from? There was more questions that didn't have answers.

 The girl sat there feeling a little bit of excitement as the man continued to talk about these horses clearly there was respect for them. This had all pretty well explained to her several questions that had been whirling around in her thoughts, but what about the three other mares where had they came from? The man took a deep breath then let it out then he said" as for the three mares that got away, it is probably best if I go all the way back to the beginning". You see way back in 1933 the U S Calvary started what was to become known as the "Remount Program". What they would do is they would provide ranchers with very high quality stallions to cross on their more native mares then the army would buy these horses to go into their Calvary replacements. The stallions were mostly Thoroughbred and Morgan horses at least that was what was here". "This place here" the man gesturing with his arm out stretched pointing to the barn and all of the corrals "was one of the last remount stations to be shut down." It had lasted several years longer than all of the rest because the man that owned it had some of the best mares of anywhere. Unlike most of the other Remount stations where the ranchers would only cross the Remount stallions with native mares, this man was first a "Horseman" and second a rancher. He had went back east and had bought enough Morgan mares to fill two railroad cars and had them shipped out west to the nearest shipping point and from there they were trailed here. He had been very particular about what he bought they were of best breeding and conformation. He was even concerned with the color, one of the prerequisites for the Calvary. They only liked to buy bays, blacks, and brown horses with very little white, so that is what the mares were that he brought here.

The army always bought his horses first and gave him a premium as well. Since the army only bought geldings that left all of the fillies to be sold at private treaty. People would come from all over just to buy a filly from here. His horses were famous for their quality in many of the surrounding states and Canada. Of course this man would always keep the very best for his own use and replacements, always making his mare bands better and bringing in new stallions to cross on the replacements. He was also a very good businessman with a good education, but mostly he liked good horses and he was passionate about raising the very best.

Because the man was a good business man whenever he saw that the army was leaving the use of horse for the more advanced machinery such a jeeps, trucks and tanks. He knew that the demand for his horses by the army would soon be coming to an end there for he needed to be looking at other areas to market his horses. Part of his plan was to decrease the numbers that he had been running. The first thing that he did was to sell off a large portion of his brood mares, keeping only the very best. Since he had a list of people that wanted to buys his horses for their own use or just to raise their own horses he contacted them all. Soon people were coming from all over to buy these animals. It seemed that the hills were bare after all of the horses had been gathered and sold to these people. Some people would only take one or two, but there were several larger ranches that would take fifteen or twenty at time, in no time at all the glory days of the Remount Station was only a thing in the past. Only one band of mares remained to roam the slopes where once hundreds of horses could be seen. Soon white face cattle took the place of the horses.

The man paused for a few moments thinking about things from the past, then he went on "the three are direct decedents of this remaining band of mares and sired by one of the best stallions that the ranch ever had. What a great horse he was and there were many colts from him that went on to be great horses. In some ways this little bunch of horses were the final chapter of one of the greatest horse endeavors ever created. The vast majority of all the western horses today can be traced back to these re-mount stallions. The two brown mares where some of his last fillies, the bay mare was a year older she was the last foal out of one of the best producing mares that was here. Her mare was a very old mare and died before time for her to be weaned so she had been brought in and fed supplement grain and hay until she had caught up with the foals. Because she was behind in a lot of ways she wound up being put with the next years crop of foals. She soon was in charge of that group. The foals were always brought in close in the winter time and supplemented with hay from the meadows down below the creek. After they had been weaned and were doing well on their own they would all be brought in taught to lead and have their feet handled. Most of them were pretty gentle to be around and a few even like to have their necks and backs scratched. The bay mare was not one that wanted to be scratched she was independent and always kept her distance. Come spring the colts were branded, the horse colts were gelded, then everything would be moved up into the highest country where they learned to be horses, they would stay there until their two year old year then they would be gathered and brought in to be started under saddle.

Shortly after this bunch of colts had been brought in to be started under saddle this man showed up wanting to buy some fillies. This was a bit of a windfall for some one to be looking for that many fillies this time of year, mostly when a buyer showed up they were looking for geldings. Normally the owner would have his pick out of the bunch and everything else would be for sale, but this time this fellow had showed up out of the blue unannounced. It sort of took everyone by surprise. Of course the owner was a businessman so he did not turn this man away, he figured he would just put a price on his pick and it would be so much higher than everything else that nobody would want to buy them. Problem solved. So as the two men were walking among the colts the owner was careful not to point out his pick which as it turned out he always kept a few fillies for the ranch. In this case they were an older bay filly and two brown ones. They walked around in the corral looking at the colts and talking, when finally the buyer ask about these other three fillies. Of course the owner quickly told him that he wasn't interested in selling them, but the man was president until finally the owner quoted him a price a very high price, to which the man said those are the ones I want. At that point the owner had to concede to the buyer. So the deal was made and the money changed hands, the three fillies were separated and arrangements were made for the man to have his truck come pick them up. The fillies would be going to the other side of the mountains about a hundred and fifty miles as the crows flies. About two hundred and fifty by way of road. There they would be put into a breeding program raising horses for a large ranch that this man had recently bought. He would be back by the end of the following week to pick them up.

Early the following week the weather took a turn for the worse it had moved in and the sky was filled with low heavy dark clouds and I began to rain, a lot. True to his word the man showed up to pick up the three fillies, along with him was his new foreman who was driving the new bobtail truck. The truck was covered with the dark mud from coming up the muddy road, but underneath it was a shiny blue with a white roof the stock racks were black with white pen stripping. The stock racks had high solid sides with a partial cover over the front half. This was good it would give the fillies some protection from the rain on the drive back. They backed it up to the loading chute and the fillies were brought down the alley and put on to the truck, everyone shook hands and they were gone. Even though the owner had gotten almost twice what he priced all of the rest of the fillies for he was sad to see this bunch of fillies leave.

It was about three weeks before word reached the head of the valley: After the three fillies were loaded the new owner and his foreman pulled away from the loading chute making the beginning of the six hour trip around to the other side of the mountains. Everything had went good until they were on the other side of the mountain well into their trip and almost to the ranch that is where things turned bad real fast. They had left the black-top and were making their way up the twenty two miles of winding mountain dirt road. The rain had been relentless and the road was a slick muddy mess, on one of the switch backs the foreman driving the bobtail with the three fillies on board had lost control and slide off of the road into a ravine. The truck had over turned and slide part way down then rolled several time to the bottom. The foreman had managed to stay in the truck but the owner was thrown out and the truck rolled over him killing him instantly. The foreman had stayed in the truck but had drown when the truck went into the muddy water that filled the bottom of the canyon. As for the three fillies they were no where to be found. The heavy rain had washed out any tracks or sign that the fillies might have left. With all of the turmoil that followed with family members and lawyers, things went into a huge tailspin. In order to satisfy all of the people that were involved the court ordered that the ranch be put up for sell. There were so many bigger more important things to deal with the fillies fell through the cracks, it didn't seem like anybody really cared about what they might have been hauling in the truck, so they were soon completely forgotten. No one even made an attempt to go in search for them to see if there were any of them crippled or injured. To everyone involved they never even existed. The fillies were on their own.

By the time news of all of this had reached back to the head of the valley the starting of the two year olds was in full swing. It also turned out the owner and his wife had just recently left for a six week tour with some fellow ranchers to Australia and New Zealand. He was to be gone for at least six weeks maybe as long as two months. There were a couple of the men that were starting the colts that did some speculation and did consider going that way to look for the fillies, but nothing ever came of it. The cattle work went on and they continued to start and ride colts. From time to time someone would bring up the subject of the three fillies wondering if they might have surfaced somewhere yet but it was as if the mountains had swallowed them up. No word of any sightings ever came and as time went on more things took their place for the people to be concerned about and they were forgotten.

Keith sat there on the tree stump with a far away look in his eyes, there had been a lot of crazy turn of events that happened after that truck pulled away from that loading chute. He sat there in silence the young girl could not think of anything to say, she had gotten way more information than she had ever imagined. Samantha had been pretty sure that this man would know something about this little band of wild horses, but a story like this she hadn't been prepared for. Finally she became aware of where she was and that the sun was already well into the western sky. Samantha stood up and thanked Keith for taking the time to talk with her, he nodded his head and stood up as well. He offered her another drink from the cool water running through the trough. She accepted the drink and as she turned to her bike the man thanked her for coming and telling him about the horses, he said that maybe he could come by sometime soon and she could show him where the horses were at he would like to see them. Samantha nodded as she climbed on her bike that would be good.

As Samantha peddled her bike out onto the dirt road her mind was already spinning with everything that she had heard today. Her little band of wild horses were really not wild after all mostly the were just forgotten. There was a breeze that was coming off of the mountain and it was very cool along with it were some heavy low hanging clouds that were hovering around the higher peaks, it felt like there was a change in the weather coming real soon. She peddled a little bit fast as she made her way down into the valley and by the time she rode into her yard the wind was well past a breeze. She hurried up and did her outside chores getting into the house as quickly as possible. Her mother already had a fire going in the big wood stove, it felt good.

As the night went on the wind grew stronger, the window to her room would shake and rattle every so often when a big gust would hit. When it first started it sounded like small pebbles hitting the window as it got stronger she could see the white stuff sticking to the screen outside the window. It was going to be a nasty night to be out, she hoped that the little band of horses would be alright. This time of year the weather could change so fast.

CHAPTER
Four

The three fillies were standing head to tail under the lean to next to the big hay rack full of fresh hay for the most part they remained dry in spite of the heavy rain that had been falling for the last two days. That is where they were when the young cowboy came into the corral he was wearing a long yellow slicker as he came up under the lean-to the fillies all gave him the big-eye and snorted as he walk to them. With very little effort the fillies swarmed out into the muddy corral running around looking at the cowboy as if he was something very scary. He herded them into the alley then down the alley up to the loading chute onto the truck that was waiting. There was some talking among the humans then the truck roared to life and they were shaken around in this small enclosure that they had been pushed into. The truck moved out onto the dirt road that let to the barn where they had been standing and as the truck drove down the road they could seen the big barn growing smaller as they went.

At first the fillies were more frightened than anything then as they got use to it the got more comfortable with the movement of the truck and in a couple of miles they were able to get their legs under themselves and get used to the moving of the truck, sometimes it would slide sideways then come back quick and they would be shuffled around but as the road got better so did the ride. After reaching the asphalt the truck smoothed out and the fillies were able to get more stable in the back, there was a part that was covered and they crowed under that staying out of the chilly rain that continued to fall. They road this way for several hours when the felt the truck make a hard turn and they felt it go back onto a slippery muddy road again. The road was very windy and there was a lot of going and coming down, this kept the fillies always braced and swaying with the movement of the truck. They were doing pretty good considering all of the swaying back and for when they were going down an incline with a sharp curve at the bottom. That is when things took a turn for the worse, the truck slide sideways hitting something very solid causing the fillies to all slam into the side panel of the truck which had kept sliding sideways and sinking in the soft mud. Along with speed of the truck the momentum kept everything going off of the road and sliding down the embankment. The next thing the truck turn over on it's side still sliding down the embankment, throwing the three fillies out of the open part of the stock racks. The fillies all landed in a big pile, tangled up and scrambling to get to their feet all the while being in each others way, as they were floundering and sliding down the slope they managed to stay away from the truck that was also going down the slope on it's side. As the fillies all got their feet under themselves and started to out run the truck it began to roll and continued to do so until it splashed into the rushing water at the bottom.

   The fillies managed to stay together as they to landed in the cold dark water that was moving so fast at the bottom of the canyon. They were slammed around by the force of the water bumping into boulders and down trees as they were swept away by the current of the water. Struggling the fillies made it to the other side of the canyon a couple of hundred yards below the truck scared, bruised, cold, wet and completely confused the fillies went up the slope of the canyon as fast as they could make it over the rugged terrain. The fillies continued to move as the evening came on and as the night came in, they moved until the terrain, darkness and exhaustion had forced them to stop. There they stood huddled in a small group each one touching the other looking for comfort and reassurance, there they stayed heads down tails tucked shivering as the cold rain continued to fall on their backs and the sound of the rushing water at the bottom of the canyon.

Some time in the predawn hours the rain began to let up and as it began to get light it lessened to just a sprinkle, there was a thick fog that had moved in and had engulfed the entire mountain. With coming of the dawn the fillies started to stir around the bay filly moved off slowly picking her way as she continued to climb up the slope, the other four followed her lead. With the adrenaline worn off and being still for so long in the cold rain the fillies all were stiff and sore from being thrown out of the truck and scrambling down the ravine. The two brown fillies were limping one on a front leg and the other was favoring a hind leg, one had a big gash down her forehead, the bleeding had stopped the rain had washed it clean. There were other cuts and scrapes but nothing as bad. They were on a very rocky steep slope that was cover in timber, the downfall was everywhere and the wet pine needles that covered the ground made the going slick and unsafe. Even so the bay continued to climb up the slope stopping to catch her breath and waiting for the others to catch up to her then she would continue on, she wanted as far as she could get from this place.

The thick fog and the wet timber muffled any sound the fillies made it was like they were ghostly shadows moving in the fog. Because of the poor soil and the pine needles that covered the ground there was hardly any grass to speak of, what little grass that they did find was very coarse and of poor quality. Sometimes they would nibble on the tough grass but it was not enough to make them stop for more than a few minutes. When the fillies finally reached the top of the slope it was little more than a long finger of a ridge, to go off the other side it was much the same as where they had just came from. By following the ridge the ground was flatter without so much downfall and the going was easier the slight incline was not as steep as climbing the slope had been. The fillies were hungry having not had any thing since they left the lean-to with the hay rack full of fresh hay. They really wanted to stop and graze, but there was no place to stop. The ridge was a rocky gravelly mix that was good for travel but had nothing in the way of feed for the fillies. The rain had all but stopped but the fog hung thick and damp the fillies dripped from the moisture of the fog and their own sweat. They came to a layer of flat rock that had pools that were full of fresh rain water, here the fillies stopped and drank they stayed by the pools until their thirst had been satisfied.

The water had freshened them up and given them new energy but they were still hungry. The bay filly moved off again the ground was getting flatter and wider the mud was deeper, they seemed to be moving onto a more open area. When they finally came out of the trees they found themselves surrounded by thick fog, but their feet were surround by thick lush fresh green grass. Their heads dropped as if they were connected, here they stopped. The fillies had traveled for the better part of the day when they came out into the meadow there wasn't much daylight left. The fillies grazed into the darkness the fog still hanging like a thick blanket over the meadow. When they had satisfied their hunger for the time being anyway they moved back into the thick timber and there they rested for the first time since leaving the lean-to.

The thick fog lay heavy, all of the night the fillies huddled together in the thick timber using each other for warmth and reassurance, their muscles ached and their bruised bodies filled every breath, they were close to exhaustion. Finding the meadow and filling up their bellies came at just the right time for them, the two lame fillies had been falling further behind as the day had worn on. They were tired and every step had been painful, but they had not stopped, that was not in their DNA. Generations of selective breeding had made them continue on even though each step they took could have been their last, even though they were beyond tired and lame they never stopped. The two lame fillies laid down in the damp pine needles in the thick timber their exhausted limbs quivering, could not hold them up any longer. The bay filly stood watch over them as they slept, she to slept but only for short periods of time. The cold, damp, foggy night seemed to go on forever.

As the morning crept into the timber the fillies started to stir they were tired and sore from the previous days travel. The two lame fillies struggles to stand but they managed to get up and stand long enough to get the circulation going again. Slowly they moved from the timber out into the lush grass of the meadow, the thick fog continued to lay across the meadow. The fillies dropped their heads and began to graze their hunger was back as the fillies grazed the morning light moved in making things brighter and easier to see, somewhere in the fog they could hear the rushing of a stream not far away. As the sun made it's way up it began to burn off the fog, streaks of sun laced fog shown through the trees and as the sun moved higher, the fog gave way to the warmth of the sun and finally the fog lifted and exposed the whole meadow that the fillies had wondered into.

The meadow was a nice size, it was in a basin that encompassing several hundred acres all covered with lush green grass. The stream near where the fillies had entered the meadow came out from underneath a big boulder, it flowed across the near side of the meadow down into the bottom of the basin then joining up with other same springs flowed into a drainage the disappeared into the timber. There was a tall jagged peak the rose up out of the meadow covered with huge boulders and gnarled stunted trees, there were several huge boulders that littered the meadow having rolled down from the steep ridge eons ago when the mountain was young. The grass was fresh, green and full of nourishment, the fillies were intent on grazing eating as much of the fresh grass as the stomachs could hold. They were hungry the last couple of days had left them empty and gaunt. As the sun moved higher in the sky it's warm began to replace the damp cold that had come with the rain and the fog, when the fillies filling up on the fresh green grass they went to the stream and took a long drink of the cold refreshing water, then they went back to more grazing. One by one the fillies stopped grazing and let the sun's warmth soak into their bodies pushing out all of the cold and wet the had been there for the last few days, soon they were all stretched out flat on the now warm green grass in a deep slumber.

The fillies slept passed midday the summer sun warming the tired and sore muscles as they slept, there was hardly any movement from any of the fillies they had been close to exhaustion and now they were slowly replacing their energy with fresh green grass, rest and warmth from the sun. The fillies slowly began to stir they did groaned and set up looking as if they had been in some sort of deep trans as they rose to their feet they left their bed of grass now flat from the weight of their bodies. The sides of the fillies were damp from the grass, with imprints of the underlying bed of meadow floor showing on their damp sleek sides. The fillies stood for a bit then stretched moved off stiffly and began to graze again. They grazed until the sun had disappeared in the western sky before moving back into the thick timber as the cool night air filled the meadow.

With the dawning of the new day the fillies having had the rest and nourishment from the bounty of the meadow the previous moved out into the meadow ready to embrace a new day, they began grazing as soon as they were out into the meadow. They were grazing when the sun made it's appearance in the morning sky pushing the cold morning air out as it filled the basin with it's warmth. For the first few days the fillies did pretty much the same thing everyday, slowly their tired a sore muscles began to recover the two lame fillies continued to improve as the days past. The fillies grazed undisturbed for several days.

It came early one afternoon the fillies had been grazing as usual but today the clouds started rolling in over the high peak the wind that rushed ahead of it was considerably cooler and there was a rumble in the sky. The first bolt of lightening to strike was less than a quarter of a mile from the fillies, striking a tall old pine tree near the edge of the timber. The flash and the crash of thunder seemed to come at the exact same instant scaring the fillies into a panic. They broke into a run all at the same time heading for the thick timber. The freezing rain and sleet that followed pushed them deeper into the comfort of the thick timber. There the fillies found refuse shivering from the cold rain and trembling and jumping from every crash of thunder. There were several trees along the edge and up above the had the twisted scar the results of a direct hit from a bolt of lightening. This became the normal thing for the afternoons and as fast as it had came it went across the mountains laving the trees and grass dripping from the sudden downpour, and then the sun was out like nothing had ever happened.

Early one morning the fillies moved out into the meadow and they were greeted with a strange new smell, as they snorted as they sniffed the cool predawn air. With the coming of the dawn they were able to see that a herd of strange creatures had come into the basin, the elk were everywhere it was a herd of cow elk and their calves. They were grazing across the basin looking like strange high headed horses in the early light. The elk stayed on the far side of the basin and the fillies stayed on the side that they had claimed as their own. As the days past the two lame fillies improved more everyday, soon they were moving around as sound as before the wreck. With the appearance of the elk and being in the basin slowly the memory of the ranch were they had been raised became a distant memory, and like the fog lifting out of the basin on a damp morning the memory of the truck rolling down the ravine came to pass as well.

Curiosity finally over came the fillies, they moved in to check out the elk one afternoon, the elk seemed have little concern for the fillies as they moved among the herd and soon the fillies began grazing along with the elk. This became a normal part of the day for the fillies and the elk to move about grazing next to each other. This was how the summer went for he fillies, they grew fat and slick on the strong mountain grass and as the smell of fall moved into the basin all of the wounds the fillies had received from the truck rolling down the ravine had healed. They were all as sound as the day they were put onto the truck and left the ranch. They had been accepted into elk herd, they moved around with the elk as they grazed during the day, they learned the ways of the elk sounding the alarm if there happened to any kind of threat to the herd, and they would bed near them at night.

As the leaves on the Aspens turned to gold the chill of fall moved into the basin. With the change came the bull elk, they moved in with their bugling and fighting for dominance in the heard. It seemed that peace and tranquility that been in the basin for so long had gone by the way of the summer sun. The morning light usually came with the bull elk fighting tearing up the frosty grass shattering the stillness that had been the normal of the basin. Their heavy breath and hot bodies making steamy clouds as the sun would make it way into the basin. The mornings were frosty and the fillies found warmth from the morning sun standing next to the big boulders that were scattered around the basin. There they would stand soaking up the morning sun letting it drive out the chill from the night before.

Late one afternoon heavy dark clouds rolled in over the peak with them came a cold wind that began whipping everything in the basin bending the tops of the tall pines, the temperature dropping like the leaves from the trees. The cold was bone chilling soon the wind was filled with heavy snow, the fillies turning tail to the wind let it push them into the heavy timber, there they found themselves surrounded by the elk. There was no more fighting the weather had moved everything into the thick timber to escape the harsh chill that had come with the wind. The animals all stood together the wind swirling the snow around them covering them with a layer of snow, the snow sticking to the hair and the warmth from their bodies soon the snow began to insulate the animals from the cold. The storm raged on all through the night and into the next day, finally near the end of the next day in began to weaken and slowly the wind quit and there was just some snow falling and soon even that stopped. All of the animals in the timber were covered with a heavy blanket of snow.

The grass the had once covered the floor of the basin was buried under a thick layer of white snow the boulders surrounded by huge drifts of snow. Slowly the animals began shaking off the thick layer of snow that was on their backs. Their backs were wet from snow that had melted and soon that to was frozen giving them a blanket of frost that helped to keep them warm from the cold. The elk pushed around in the deep snow looking for some of the grass that had been covered, soon one of the old lead cows moved away making her way through the snow. The rest of the herd followed behind the old cow and soon there was a deep trail in the snow going down country. The fillies fell in with the elk following them as they made they way into lower country and by early morning the elk and the fillies all walked out into a wide valley full of grass. They had left the basin and all of it's bitter cold for this lower valley.

As the winter wore on the fillies stayed among the elk, following them learning were to find the best grass and open waters. The fillies no long had the sleek summer coats they traded those for thick, heavy coats of long hair, with this and the dry cured grass that they found in the lower country they were able to withstand the wind and the harsh cold that the winter brought.

CHAPTER *Five*

The days got longer and as they did the sun became stronger making the days warmer, many days would find the fillies next to the timber lounging in the sun letting the cold that had crept into their bodies during the night be replaced by the warm rays from the sun. Slowly the snows began to melt during the day and freezing back during the nights, by day the ground became muddy and frozen at night. As the waters and the ponds backed up by beaver damns became to open up the skies began to fill with V's of geese and other water fowl on their way north to their summer homes. The birds would stay a few days resting and feeding on the beaver ponds and then they would be gone again. The Red Wing black birds filled the areas where the reeds and cattails stood, chirping and fluttering feeding in the open ground behind the fillies and the elk. Soon the snow turned to mud and the shallow streams became full and swift making it difficult to cross in many places. Slowly the icy fingers of winter began to let go and the more gentle fingers of spring took their place.

The long heavy coats of hair that the fillies had grown for the cold's of winter began to turn loose, the hair began to itch making the fillies look for places to rub and dry places to roll leaving the ground covered with clumps of hair. The fillies had lost lost their roundness and their sides were flat letting some of their ribs be seen under their hide. As the days got warm shoots of green grass found it's way out in the sunny places and under the edge of the melting snow. The fillies went after this new growth of grass with a hunger that they had never had before. The elk to were going after the fresh grass causing them to break up into smaller groups grazing farther out everyday, soon many of them moved on looking for more of the green grass. The fillies to began to move farther and farther from the valley that had kept them safe for the winter grazing and drifting always looking for fresh green grass. The green grass soon was more than a few shoots in a sunny place, it was coming up everywhere making a short green carpet across the floor in the bottom of the wide canyon that they had drifted into. The water was good and the grass was getting better by the day fillies finished shedding their patchy winter coat and their shinier summer coat took it's place the fillies began to gain back the weight that they had used up during the winter. They began buck and play, the green grass had them feeling lively once again.

There was something stirring in the fillies that made them continue to be on the move. One evening the fillies having filled up on green grass and water began drifting up a ridge leaving their canyon that had been filled with good grass and fresh water. They began traveling following an old game trail head to tail the bay filly in the lead. The moon was full when the fillies reached the top of the ridge out of the canyon they moved through the night crossing a couple more canyons working their way up the next ridge. The light of the full moon made the travel cool and easy shining like a filtered sun. The fillies stopped and grazed in a small canyon covered in fresh with a nice spring full of cool water. The water came from under a big rock with a twisted pine tree growing out of a crack in the rock. Here the fillies grazed filling the bellies with the fresh grass drinking water and rested for much of the day. The fillies traveled for two more days stopping and grazing and resting when they came upon a good place to do so.

Early one evening they came off the end of a long ridge that went out into a big grass covered flat, the flat was several miles long and many more wide it was the biggest open country the fillies had ever been in. With no trees or rocks and nothing but openness the fillies were a bit uneasy for a while. Following a trail the fillies came to a windmill just as darkness of night set in, snorting softly they walked around smelling and looking the water in the drinking tub smelled different than any they had ever smelled before. It had a bit of a stale smell about it, but finally the fillies gave way to their thirst and drinking and spooking scaring each other but, finally they finished drinking and as they were smelling around they could tell that other horses had been using the water, there was also some salt blocks laying near the windmill. Not having any salt since before they had been put on the truck the cold rainy day so long ago they went to the salt licking and gnawing with their teeth to satisfy the craving that built up with them. After eating salt and drinking water then eating more salt dawn found the fillies content but hungry, following another trail they worked their way out on the grassy flats that surrounded the windmill. Morning found them heads down filling up on the tall grass up wind from the windmill. The windmill was turning lazily in the slight breeze the water almost making it to the pipe to drain into the drinking trough then the breeze would stop the water waiting for the next breeze to finish bringing it to the top to spill into the pipe that went into the metal trough.

The fillies were head down, the breeze moving the tall grass around their heads when the big roan stallion appeared out of nowhere. He was in the middle of them before they even realize that there was another horse so close. The fillies scattered snorting and nickering running in different directions then circling back around heads and tails in the air prancing then stopping and snorting loud snorts almost like a loud whistle. The big stallion standing in the middle head and tail high he too was snorting and nickering. The fillies continued to run around the roan stallion coming in closer smelling and snorting finally coming in close to the big roan stallion, smelling noses the stallion squealed and the filly spun around kicking the stallion with both hind feet. It was a solid hit in the ribs of the old stallion, the stallion spinning around and sending some kicks back to the fillies. The excitement went on for well over an hour the fillies landing more kicks and the stallion doing the same, by the end of the day they were all sore and missing patches of hair from their sides and necks.

The stallion was an old horse well past his prime, one of his knees was permanently swollen and stiff and after the day of battering excitement with the fillies he was stiff and sore. The stallion belonged to the ranch that was a few miles away back under a big rim rock. The stallion had found a wire gate that had been left open probably by some hunter and had went out late last fall, him and his mare band had always been put at the windmill and that was home to him. Being and old horse there had not been a lot of concern when he wasn't found in the pasture that he had been put in. The old horse had spent the winter alone at the windmill living the solitary life. It had been a big excitement for him when he came into the windmill for water and picked up the smell of the fillies. Like the fillies he had not seen another horse for several months.

The old stallion took control of the little band of fillies he reinforced his role with severe bites on the necks and rumps of the fillies, he was soon herding them around taking them to grass and bringing them into water. They had settled into their roles and the fillies had put on more fat as the grass grew greener the old roan stallion lost some of his fat working to keep the fillies under his control. Everything had been as good as it could be the fillies had finally gotten their fill of the salt blocks and they had gotten use to the strange smell and taste of the water from the windmill.

One day in the middle of the afternoon the little band of horses heard a high pitched sound of a motor, the old stallion knew what the sound was but the fillies had never heard this kind of a motor before. The motor grew louder and the fillies grew nervous and when the motor came into view it stopped. It was a motorcycle the rider stopped and looked at the little band of horses then he started moving slowly around the band. The fillies were more nervous now than they had ever been as the motorcycle began trying to maneuver around and keep the fillies with the stallion they became more excited. One or two of them would dart out and the motorcycle would circle around to bring them back, finally the fillies could not take it any longer and they all broke out at the same time scattering in three different directions, but all heading back for the long ridge that they had followed in to the big flat. The old stallion handicapped with age and a bad knee ran nickering as far as he could not wanting to loose his little band of fillies. The fillies being young and athletic from the combination of good genetics and having lived in the steep mountains all of their lives ran as if they had wings. The man on the motor bike riding for all he was worth was still no match for the fillies. It was almost like the motor bike was about to get the advantage over the fillies getting them bunched and was in the process of getting to the lead to start to turn them back toward the old stallion and the windmill, when the gully got in the way of that. The man on the bike was going so fast with most of his attention focused on the fillies that he neither saw nor had time to react. The bike went into the gully and out the other side the engine racing even louder when the motor bike went several into the air landing in a pile bouncing and rolling to a stop the rider landing several feet away also bounced and rolled. The dust was thick and still hung in the air when the ranch hand got to his hands and knees there was so much air and he could not get any of it his shoulder hung down from where it normally was and one side of his ribs wear screaming with pain, he was sure that he had broken his collar bone and some ribs. If he could just get some air back into his lungs he could maybe get to his feet, he was scrapped and bruised as well and along with his pride the motorbike was broke as well. He was in for a slow, long, painful walk back to the ranch, there he would have to explain how he wrecked the ranch's motorbike. The old stallion had given up on the chase and he stood watching his little band of mares getting smaller as the ran for the long ridge.

The fillies continued to run even though the machine had stopped chasing them there had been a big cloud of dust and then it was quiet but fillies ran on. The fillies were a bout winded when they reached the bottom of the long ridge their nostrils were flared drinking in the wind, their hearts pounding in their chests and their sides covered with sweat they started the long climb back up the ridge. The fillies fell into line as they started up the long ridge the bay filly in the lead, the two brown fillies heads down side heaving fell into line behind her. The bay mare led them up the ridge to where the scrub trees began there she finally stopped the sweat running off their sides and down their legs dripping from the longer hair at there pasterns onto the ground. Their sides heaving their nostrils drinking in as much air as they could and the legs shaking, they stood for a while until they were able to move on.

CHAPTER
Six

The fillies had stood there until they had gotten their wind back the sweat had started to dry when the bay filly went again she continued to go up the ridge as the sun disappeared on the horizon. The bay filly never faltered she had no desire to return to the windmill. The little band of fillies traveled through the night retracing the route that had taken them to the big flat and the windmill. In the early hours of dawn the fillies came to a small canyon with fresh grass there was some small pools of water gathered from recent rains. There the fillies drank the fresh cool water and began grazing they had not been this exhausted since that night now an almost forgotten memory of the truck rolling down the ravine. The fillies grazed until midday then with warm sun they rested even laying down and sleeping. The fillies started to stir as the shadows were getting long, the went back to the pools drank their fill of water again grazed til the sun was gone then they were on their way again. The fillies continued on for the better part of two days only stopping for water and grazing for a while then they would move on again.

When the fillies came to the canyon that had the fresh green grass and the spring that came from under a big rock with the twisted pine tree growing out of it they dropped their heads and grazed. They tired foot sore and hungry, Here they grazed and drank the fresh spring water for several days. Here they seemed to feel safe from the loud engine of the motorbike and the constant control of the old roan stallion. The grass in the canyon was lush and strong here the fillies flanks filled out again and the sweat marks gave way to the shiny coats the fillies had found a good place to recover from their experience out in the big flat.

After a couple of weeks in the canyon the grass began to play out the fillies were having a harder time keeping their bellies full, early one afternoon after drinking from the spring the bay filly began walking out of the canyon. The two brown fillies fell in behind and soon they were stringing across the next ridge head to tail stepping out climbing higher with every step. The fillies continued moving always going high and deeper into the mountains, they would only stop to graze and to drink water when the found it. The little band moved like this for several days until early one afternoon they moved out into the basin beneath the tall peak with the big boulders scattered around the bottom, lush grass and the stream that came out from under a big rock. The bay mare had led them back to the basin where they had spent the last summer. Summer was well under way by the time they made it back this time. The cow elk and their calves were already occupying the basin the calves were no longer laying everywhere, they were spending most of their time in playing in little groups or moving and grazing with the cows. The thunderstorms that came along the rest of the summer were loud and violent with lightening striking several of the cow elk. Several more trees became the victim of the lightening that summer show a bright yellow twisted scar that would go down the trunk into the ground. Some of them had the tops blown completely off making the top fall to the ground.

The fillies made good use of their days in the basin grazing on the strong green grass and drinking the cool fresh water that came from under the big rock. As the summer began to pass and the grass began to cure, as some would say the "bottom fell" out of the fillies. Their girths deepened and they had a growth spurt in what seemed like over night the fillies became mares they were much bigger standing 15/2 or taller the smallest weighing 1250 pounds or better. They were a very impressive looking set of horses all very straight and correct, they were smooth, quick, and athletic when they moved.

As the summer gave way to fall the Quaking Aspen leaves turned to gold some falling to the ground looking like gold coins lying on the grass. The grass continued to cure turning a dull yellow color the morning's covering it with a heavy frost. The bull elk began moving to the basin with their loud grunts and high pitched bugling they came in. The days were filled the commotion that came with bulls chasing cows and fighting other bulls was what they did everyday. The days grew shorter and the temperature continued drop, but the heavy snow didn't come, there were only a few flurries and light dusting's of snow. The temperature continued to drop even further the days sunny and extremely cold the nights going even colder. The mares and the elk had hung on until early one afternoon the wind began to blow at first just a cold wind the with a huge gust the temperature took a huge drop moving the elk and the mares deep into the timber. The wind did not let up through the night forcing the temperature way down into the minuses, but still no snow only a bitter wind.

Before dawn could break the elk and the mares were on the move they were doing their best to stay in front of this bitter cold that had taken over. The wind keep the two groups moving pushing heir way down into the lower valley, hunting relief they moved further down into the lower country going even further then the winter grounds they used the winter before. They went until they found a long open flat the was kind of protected form the bitter wind, it had a southern slope so they could move up into the sun when it was coming over the ridge first thing in the mornings. Here they took refuse from the wind that seemed blow everyday only bringing more cold. The flat that they had come to was on the edge of cattle grazing country so the grass had seen grazing earlier in the fall so it was not the fresh kind of grass that they were so used to. The was slow moving freezing up most of the time so everything was in competition for a drink. The mares stayed for a few days growing tired of having to fight off so many elk for a drink they moved on braving the relentless wind that they seemed to never have a break from.

The bay mare took the lead quartering into the wind they they made the climb the cold wind sucking out their breath as the went. When they finally reached the crest and crossed over the top starting to drop into the other side they seemed have finally gotten a break from the wind. As they made their way down the sloped into the next canyon the wind seemed to blow over them not so much right into them. When they reached the bottom there lots of fresh grass but no water. Tired and cold from the trek across the big ridge they dropped their heads and grazed into the darkness of the coming night. Daylight came with a stiff frigid breeze coming off of the top. The mares grazed for a while, but their thirst was growing. The bay mare took the lead heading for the opposite slope, the two brown mares fell in behind her head to tail.

When the mares were making their way back to the basin after being chased out of the flats by the motorbike a couple of days after leaving the canyon with spring coming out from under a big boulder with a twisted tree growing out of it, they had come across another canyon. It had deep sides mostly of sheer rock with only a few places that could be climbed out of or down into. The canyon floor was flat and wide with lots of fresh grass, there was water there to pools under the steep rims gathered but did not flow. The mares had spent only a couple of days in this canyon they had been determined to make their way back to the basin were they had spent the summer before.

When the mares finally came to rim of the steep canyon they walked up and down the ridge before deciding on a path to take to reach the bottom of the canyon. The trail was steep and cover with loose rocks of all sizes some of good size. As the mares made their way down they started little rock slides some of the rocks reaching the bottom before they could, when the last mare trotted onto the canton floor rocks were still rolling down behind her. The mares found relief from the bitter cold wind when they came into the bottom of this canyon with the high steep walls. When they made their way to where the pools of water were they found them to be froze over with a thin layer of ice. As soon as one pawed at the ice it caved in leaving the pool open allowing them to drink. It was the first drink of water that they had been able to get in two days.

The snows never came that winter, only the relentless bitter wind the seemed blow everyday and every night. Down in the canyon the winds seldom made it to the canyon floor. The mares grazing on the good grass and drinking from the pools of water were content and lounged in the sun next to the steep rock walls of the canyon. The cold winter had found it's place and seemed reluctant to recede into spring.

The bitter Alberta Clippers continued one behind the other only bringing bitter cold winds never any snow, the temperatures seldom climbing above zero. Many animals to old or sick or just to young, lives were claimed by the brutal winter, the bitter cold to much for their frail bodies to withstand. The mares came through in good condition due to the easy nature of the canyon with the rim walls. When one of the driest, coldest, and windiest winters finally broke the elk and the cattle that had wintered out were thin and in poor condition. Thanks to their fortunate find the mares came through in good condition. As the winter broke the sun grew warmer and the grass tried to green but there was so little moisture left in the ground that it soon gave going into it's doormat state again waiting for better times. The grass that was left in the canyon had lost most of it's nutrition so the mares were just maintaining, it was looking like it was going to be a rough spring as well.

After several days of unseasonably warm weather the air became very still almost hot, over head it was a different story the thick dark clouds were building coming in low over the mountain. Soon the long rolling thunder could be heard even away from the mountains and soon the low dark clouds covered the sky blocking out all of the sun's warmth. The thunder continued, then there was a rush of cold air that took over the canyon, with in minutes there were drops of rain hitting the ground and on the mares backs. It was only a few hitting in random places at first and then they became more steady. As the day wore on the rain continued, the dry, wind beaten ground soaking up the rain as if it had never had rain before.

The mares standing heads down tails to the rain their long heavy winter coat still in tack kept the rain from penetrating to the skin, from time to time the mares would shake their bodies sending the water back into the air and onto the ground. The rain continued mostly steady for several days when the rain did stop it remain cloudy and cool then the rain would soon begin again. While the rain was coming down where the mares were the snow in the higher terrain was falling by the foot, putting several feet of snow on the peaks and higher terrain. Mixing with the wind it had made some huge drifts in these areas. After the ground was soaked up and could hold no more it began the make pools and puddles, the lower areas began to fill up and everything was soon making it's way into the draws and drainage's it was long until everything was running with fresh rain water. The mares had retreated in the timber staying under the thick canopy of the lower branches.

After several days of low dark clouds and steady rain, the rain stopped and the sun made a small appearance, the temperature began to rise and the clouds started to open up letting more sunshine to reach the ground. Soon the clouds were drifting away and the sun took over as the sun warmed the ground steam rose from all that it's warmth touched. The mares shook the water from their backs before moving out from under the tall pines into the open where the sun was shining in full force. The sun shown all afternoon and by the time sundown came there was green tint everywhere that before had only been a dry dusty color. The mares with their heads down were going after the fresh new blades of grass with a craving that was to long overdue.

The days continued to be warm and the grass was growing so fast that you could almost hear it grow, the mares spent most of their days eating the strong fresh green grass. The long shaggy winter coat began to turn and when the mares would lay down and roll they would leave large clumps of winter hair laying in the dirt where they rolled. Underneath was the smooth silky coat of summer hair that would take them through until the leaves turned to gold and the nights were getting cold again. The mares were working hard at replacing all of the weight that they had lost over the winter. As the grass grew quickly it turned the whole countryside into a bright green color, every animal that ate grass was going after it like this might be the last time for it to be here.

The days grew warmer and the mares grazed their way back into shape they were fat and slick looking like perfect pictures of horse flesh. With the days growing warmer the nights too became milder and it wasn't long until the mares began to feel restless. Late one afternoon the bay mare walked to the rim wall looking for a way up out of their little canyon. The two brown mares fell in behind her head to tail. The heavy rain had eroded the trail out of the canyon it was a tough and difficult climb out of the canyon but they all made it to the top of the rim their side heaving and their hearts pounding in their chests, there was sweat on their necks and in their flanks. The stood for a few minutes after they reached the top catching their breath. Then they moved off once again.

CHAPTER Seven

The mares traveled most of the night stopping on occasion to graze on some grass or to drink water when it was available. The mares traveled steady for the next several days stopping once for a couple of days in a small meadow with a stream running through the middle of it. Here they grazed on the fresh grass and rested and then they were on their way once again moving up deeper into the mountains. As the mares moved into the higher country there was still snow drifts from the spring storm in many places. Sometimes they were walking in fetlock deep mud and other times they were pushing through chest high snow with deeper drifts. The days were warm but the nights were cold freezing the mud and snow at night making travel more difficult.

Finally the mares made it to the basin with the high peak and the scattered boulders with the stream coming out from under a big rock. There was still a lot of snow in the basin, there was open grass but there were snow drifts twenty feet high. The grass was only now starting to grow in the warm places where the sun reached the ground. The mares were tired from coming through the mud and pushing through the snow drifts that had been along the way. They grazed in the old damp grass from the year before not because it was good, but because they were hungry and their inter clocks said that this was were they needed to be. The mares found some green along the snow drifts, the grass was growing under the snow and as it melted it became exposed allowing the mares to get at it.

The ground was damp under the layer of old grass, slowly the sun grew stronger during the day but the nights were still very cold. As the days became longer and warmer short shoots of grass began to push up through the covering of old grass. The mares were doing much better with the green grass mixing in with the old grass. As the days got warmer the huge drifts of snow began to settle and became more packed melting along the edges. They were going to be here for a while.

The basin was covered with bright green grass with the contrasting snow drifts they were still around although not as big as they had been when the mares had first arrived. It was on one of these nice warm days that the brown mare with the white snip on her nose wondered off from the other two. She did not know why she needed to be alone, but she knew that she needed to fine a place that was warm and safe. The brown mare with the snip on her nose stay way from the other mares for three days and when she returned there was a little black filly colt pressing against her flank. This created a lot of excitement among the other two mares they came running up to her trying to sniff the new colt and get close and check her out, the brown mare with snip on her nose laid her ears back and sometimes kicking out with her hind feet keeping them pushed back until they seemed to loose interest of the new arrival. The little black filly was all legs and they were wobbly. When she would try to lay down her long legs refusing to do so and when they did finally turn loose she would flop down there she would fall into a deep sleep with her mother nearby keeping a watchful eye on her new baby.

The little black new arrival was several days old when the brown mare with the white spot in her forehead took leave of the group. She was gone for several days and when she made her return there was a little bay filly pushing against her flank as she re-joined the group. The arrival of the second filly was not as exciting as it had been for the first one, they had grown use to having a little horse in their group. As the days grew longer they grew warmer and the snow was leaving fast. The basin was greening up more everyday. The mares were picking up and putting on weight and the condition that they had lost over the long cold winter. The mares were giving lots of strong milk and the foals were growing more everyday. It had gotten much warmer during the days and the night had become milder when the bay mare left the bunch.

Just like the other two the bay was gone for several days and when she returned she two had a little black colt hugging her flank as she returned. Unlike the other two foals this one was a horse colt jet black not a white mark on him. He was long legged and wobbly, the bay mare was proud of her foal and very protective of him. With the three mares busy with their own little ones they didn't pay a lot of attention to the elk as they came into the basin with their young calves. The snow was just about all gone and the grass was growing taller everyday. The mares were slick and getting fatter with the strong grass that grew in the basin. The foals were growing fast from the rich milk that the mares were producing.

The two filly foals were getting old enough that they were starting to notice each other and they would want play, the little black foal he was young enough that he didn't get to far from his mother's side. Early one afternoon the mares were grazing near the timber line the two filly colts were bouncing around trying to play with each other, the bay mare had moved off a little ways nearer to the timber line. The black colt had laid down in some shade from the trees with the bay mare grazing near by always with one eye on the little black colt that lay asleep in the shade.

The black colt had slept for a good while, when he woke up he was no longer in the shade of the tree he was in the bright sunlight and had began to sweat on the side that was next to the ground. He had set up and was laying on his belly with his front feet out in front of him, he pushed himself to his feet still under the spell of the long sleep. That was when it happened, it happened fast and without warning. The tan tawny figure came out of the shadows of the timber through the tall grass and was on the black colt before he could even get his feet under himself. The big cat struck the colt breaking his neck in one quick swipe with his long strong claws. The colt squealed and fell dead, the bay mare was in action instantly she covered the few yards between her and the black colt in two big lounges. Her eyes were seeing red her nostrils were flared and her heart was full of hate for this thing that had attacked her baby. In the blink of an eye she was on the big cat, she had hit there so fast the cat had no time to react to her attack. The bay mare bared her teeth taking the cat by the side of the neck her powerful jaws picking the cat up and shaking him, the cat lashed out with his claws scratching at anything he could make contact with. One of the hind feet catching the bay mare along side of her neck leaving two long deep gashes in her neck, the mare slamming the cat to the ground she began to paw him with both front feet crushing bones and not letting the big cat get back to his feet he was unable to get away from this fury of teeth and hooves. The mare stomping and kicking at everything that was around her she reached in with her teeth this time gripping the ear of the big cat and ripping it and a whole mouth full if skin from the cats head and neck. The big cat screamed and the bay mare tore more skin from his body and pawed and stomped him with her front hooves until the big cat was no longer moving. She stomped on the big cat until it wasn't much more than a pile of fur and bones. The hate and fury that had come over the bay mare was slow to leave, at one point she even got down on her knees and pressed down with all of her weight on the remains of the big cat. When she finally had enough she went to the side of her colt he was laying lifeless and still, the bay mare covered in sweat, blood running down her neck and shoulder down her leg onto the ground the blood forming puddles around her feet. She tried pushing the little body with her nose to make it get up, but there was no response. The bay mare tried gently pawing at her baby to make it get up and there not any signs of life. The bay mare stood over the little lifeless body for three days and nights, the blood drying on her neck and leg the deep gashes stiff and sore, the trampled carcass of the dead mountain lion laying nearby. Finally her overwhelming thirst and need for a drink of water forced her to leave the little black body. The bay mare would come back from time to time until she finally gave up and moved away. During the fight with the mountain lion the two brown mares with foals by their sides had run to the bay mare they tried the bite and kick at the lion as the bay was biting and pawing him. They were snorting and nickering and rushing around all trying to get a bite or a kick in on the big cat. They all were very protective of the foals. It took the bay mare a few days to get over her loss she ate very little mainly just going for water, the mare lost considerable weight she spent most of her days in the darker timber avoiding the flies and other insects that preyed on her open wounds. The two brown mares would sometimes during the day gather around the bay mare and lick the open wounds cleaning away any infection their saliva acting like a healing agent for the wounds, until finally her wounds began to heal, feeling better she began to eat the tall green grass again and regain her condition.

 The summer went on with the violent thunderstorms and rain with sleet, the mares putting on plenty of weight and the foals growing and learning how to run and play across the broken ground. They were developing into a couple of nice fillies. The elk were doing the same the harsh winter before had taken a toll on the elk and there wasn't as many as there had been in the past. Even though there were still the violent thunderstorms, they weren't as numerous as they had been before and the amount of rain that fell from them was not nearly as much either. The range had become much drier in the last year and it was already staring to show on the fragile meadows of the higher country.

CHAPTER
Eight

Once again the fall came early, the leaves turning to their golden color and the mornings covered with frost. The mares and foals growing thick coats of hair for the coming winter. Soon the bull elk with all of their bugling and fighting moved into the basin and the kayaus began again. The young horses learning quickly to stay out of the way of the bulls, especially when they were fighting. Much like the previous fall the weather just turned bitter cold with very little moisture. At the very end of the fall a Norther blew in bringing cold bitter winds and blinding snow, the elk and the little band of horses were engulfed in a swirling, snow filled, bitter wind. The horse found themselves huddled up and shivering among the herd of elk in the thickest of timber once again. The young fillies learning when to hold their ground and when to give ground with the elk.

The storm blew strong and violent for several days and even though there snow with it there wasn't that much of it and it was a dry snow, not having a lot of moisture to it. After a day and half of the huddling in the thick timber one of the old elk cows moved of taking the lead, soon elk and horses were lined out single file working their way through the thick timber down into the lower country. The storm raged on in the basin and higher peaks.

The old cow was wise and had spent several winters in the lower country her little bunch of cows had joined up with some other that were on their way to the basin earlier that summer. She had never been to the basin before, but she had spent hard winters in the lower country and she knew where to go to escape the harsh, bitter winds of winter. She held the lead and kept her pace, everything else followed. The old cow held her coarse for two and a half days finally coming down a steep and rocky ridge into a wide grassy valley. The valley was probably a mile wide and several miles long, opening up into the big plains to the east. The valley was cover with good grass that had cured out making a strong feed for the elk and horses. Toward the middle of the valley was a stream that came down from the mountains, the water clear, fresh and, cold. Only the wind had reached into the valley, all of the snow that had come in the basin had stayed in the higher country. The grass was dry and open as the elk and the little band of horses came down into the valley they began scattering out, heads down grazing on the fresh grass. The wind not reaching the valley floor with it's full force and with the sun out it was a pleasant place compared to the basin that they had recently left.

The winter raged on in the higher country but it had little to no affect on the herd of elk and the little band of horse that occupied the long valley that opened up to the east. With only a few snows that didn't last for very long, the cold days of winter seemed to have no end, the elk and the horses sharing the valley on the better days and sharing the timber along the edge on the bitter windy days.

The little band of horses seemed content to stay and share the wide valley with the elk, the bay mare had found a place that fit her needs as well as the rest of the little band. As the winter wore on the upper part of the wide valley began to show the affects of the grazing from the elk along with horses, slowly they began to follow the grass toward the lower part of the valley. As they worked their way down the valley the days finally began to warm up, the mares taking advantage of the suns warmth would stand and snooze in the midday sun, sometimes they would be stretched out flat on the ground.

The days had been steadily getting warmer and there were signs of the grass trying to turn green, all of the elk and the horses were going after the fresh blades of grass almost as fast as it could grow. The results being that because there wasn't enough of the fresh green grass that they all so craved to keep their bellies full. The elk and the little band of horses began to loose weight some of the older elk with broken teeth lost a lot of their flesh that they had maintained over the winter. During one particular warm afternoon the sky began to darken with heavy dark clouds and the distant thunder moved into the valley. Soon the big cold drops of rain began to fall the mares turning their tails to wind and the rain allowed themselves to drift into the nearby timber, there they could be could of the wind and much of the rain. The rain continued to fall for the rest of the afternoon and into the night. As the night grew colder the wind stopped and the rain turned to snow, the snow was falling with big heavy flakes the valley was soon covered in a blanket of white snow. The snow muffling most of the sounds, the only sound to be heard was the sound of the snowflakes landing on and around the horses.

The little band of horses and the elk that had come into the patch of timber when that did stood and stomped around under the heavy limbs of the big trees, some of the elk laying down chewing their cuds. The snow was still coming down heavy as the dawns light came into the valley, the snow almost knee deep to the horses standing under the big trees. As the day went on so did the snow the deep snow covering the grass that had covered the valley floor for so long. As darkness fell the snow continued to fall steady and always getting deeper. The night wore on and the snow fell never letting up the horses standing heads down flanks shivering from the cold occasionally one would shake the snow from its back that was all that moved. The elk had gotten under some of the lower branches and the snow piling up on them they had a canopy under the heavy limbs until the heavy snow fell through, then they to were covered with heavy wet snow.

The snow fell heavy all night and into the morning, finally early afternoon the snow began to let up and finally coming to a stop. The sky remained dark and overcast, the temperature not improving any either. The mares stood with the heavy snow on their backs for a long time finally the bay mare shook the snow off of her back and began to stir around, the snow was deep in came up past her belly when she moved out from the treeline. The valley floor was level with the fresh white snow, the grass that had been there was nowhere to be had. The horses were hungry as were the elk that had weathered the storm next to the horses. As the bay mare pushed her way out into the open she began to paw the snow making her way down to the dry grass that had been covered by the heavy snow. The two brown mares and the filly colts followed the bay mare and soon they were pawing at the deep snow fighting for the grass underneath the heavy layer of snow. The effort was hard and the return was little but the mares were hungry and they were determined to get to the grass beneath the deep snow. The elk pushing their heads deep into the snow coming up with mouths full of grass chewing the snow covered grass as they stood there, their heads caked with heavy snow only their eyes showing through.

For the next few days it was all that any of the horses or the elk could to just get enough grass to keep themselves going, the temperature had turned cold so the snow wasn't going anywhere. The only thing it had done was settled a little bit. The mares continued to paw for every bite that they got the two fillies pawing their own grass and sometime eating along side of their mothers. The mares had weaned the fouls late in the fall biting and kicking at them until they understood that they we no longer welcome to come nurse. At first the fillies were frustrated and cranky, but they soon got over it and began their new lives of grass and browse. They had done good for themselves over the winter and now they were doing okay even though the grass was covered in a blanket of deep snow.

    Finally the hazy, heavy cold air moved out of the valley and the sun's warmth was felt again, since it was later into the spring the sun had a lot of power. It was very warm and the snow was so bright it was almost blinding. The snow began to melt settling as it did making the snow wet and heavy, pawing at the snow would only turn it into slush, but the little band of horses did the best they could their legs sore and tired and their hooves soft from the wetness of the snow. At night when the sun went down the temperature did so as well and by morning a thick hard crust had formed over the top of the snow. Sometimes it was so thick that the horses could walk on top of the snow falling through occasionally, by mid-morning the sun's warmth had it soft enough that they could continue to paw for the grass underneath. It was almost a week before patches of bare ground and grass began to be present again, as soon as the snow melted and the grass appeared it was eaten almost instantly.

    As the sun continued to melt the snow it was soaking deep into the dry ground and as the snow moved back in the bare areas the green grass was growing under the snow. The elk and the little band of horses having lost much of the remaining flesh that they had were down to hide and bones the cold and deep snow had taken it toll, several of the older elk dying not being able to make it through the cold and deep snow. The mares were gaunt and their ribs were showing the long winter coat looking shaggy and dead. The two fillies were thin and beginning to get weak as the grass began to grow, it had come just in time for them.

    Finally the snow was gone except for what was left in the shady places, the dry ground had turned into a muddy mess, the horses sinking into the mud up past their pasterns with every step. It took every bit of what little energy the animals had left just move around, the grass not grow fast enough to fill any of their bellies, just enough to make them want more. During the day the mud was deep and wet and at night it would freeze into a layer that was hard as a rock. When the mud finally did begin to dry and firm up, the horses were weak and looking very rough their eyes were dull their hooves were soft, short, and sore, the long winter coat was looking even longer with thin sides on the horses the hair looking dead almost burnt, the elk didn't look any better.

Fortunately the days got longer and warmer and the grass began to grow in such a manner that soon the valley floor was no longer a brown earth color it was turning green and getting greener everyday. The little band of horses seldom raised their heads they were so hungry and so intent on trying to eat as much of the fresh green grass as they could hold. As the days past the little band of horses continued to eat their fill of the strong tinder grass, at first their ribs showing and their bellies round from being full of fresh green grass. Slowly they began to built back the flesh and the muscle that they had lost over the winter and especially with the efforts of the deep snow. Their eyes began to look bright and alive again and when the laid down and rolled they would leave behind a carpet of thick dead winter hair. The sleek and shiny summer coat had finally arrived. When the two fillies shed off they were completely different colors the bay filly had turned into a bay roan, her head and legs up to the hocks and knees were a bay color with black points, the rest of her body a frosty reddish almost white color with a black mane and tail. The black filly had turned into a dark blue roan her head and legs remained black with a black mane and tail. They were two very classy young fillies.

With the exception of a late brutal winter storm the valley that the wise old cow elk had led them into had been paradise for the horses the winter had been mild and now the grass was over ankle deep everywhere that they stepped. The horses had accumulated their fat back and they were feeling good, the fillies running and bucking chasing the younger elk around, the deep snow and cold had been forgotten. Neither the elk nor the horse had any desire to leave the valley it was everything that they needed.

Early summer found the little band of horses still indulging in the spoils of the valley, the rains had came every week sometimes daily the grass was as good as it could get. The elk had started having their calves the cycle had started again and all was right with the world. It happened all at once and with out warning, it was a hot humid early summer day, the horses were grazing near the tree line and the elk were mostly near the stream that came from the mountains into the head of the valley. Suddenly the air was full of black gnats there were clouds of them swarming all over the horses and the elk. Getting into their eyes, into their nostrils, crawling down into their ears and biting everywhere that they landed on the animals, the peace and tranquility of the valley had been broken. The horses swishing and wringing their tails, shaking their heads, running into the timber could not get away from the annoying pest. No matter how hard they tried the black clouds of the flying demons were there. Finally night fall came and the horses got so relief from the gnats.

CHAPTER Nine

With the early light of dawn the horses came out of the thick timber and into the open valley floor, they began to graze on the green grass. They did not notice that the elk were gone they had left int night soon after the arrival of the clouds of black gnats. The horses went to the stream drank their fill of the fresh cold water and then they were back out on the valley floor grazing on the green grass. As the sun's rays began to fill the valley so did the clouds of black gnats, once again driving the little band of horses back into the thickest timber they could get into.

The little band of horses suffered through the next few days drinking water and grazing in the early mornings or late in the night. It was on a warm bright moonlit night the horses were out in the valley trying to graze but the black gnats and misquotes were covering them in swarms, the bay mares raise her head and took off in a trot the rest of the band following close behind. The bay mare headed for the head of the valley climbing up a steep rock trail that came out of the mountain down into the valley. The bay mare went up the trail and traveled into the night leaving the clouds of black gnats and the wide valley behind.

The little band of horses spent the next few days on the move, grazing and looking for water it was by no surprise that they wound up in the basin a few days later. It seemed to be the place that they always came to in in the hot summer months. There was still snow in the shady places where the wind had blown it making huge drifts, the rains had been heavy sometimes lasting for several days the ground was soft and spongy the grass was the tallest it had ever been, it was belly deep to the horses. The cow elk with their calves were as fat as they could be. Soon the little band of horses were enjoying the tall grass the two fillies were go at as if to make up for the time they lost during the deep snow. They began to grow and soon the no longer looked like two awkward pot-bellied yearling, but they were turning into two very nice looking fillies filling out and showing lots of muscle, that went well with their classy roan colors.

The rains and the violent thunderstorms continued to come through the rest of the summer the grass coming up on the sides of the three mares and over the backs of the two fillies, it was heading out and the mares had never been so fat and slick, The fillies growing taller and thicker everyday. By the end of the summer they were almost as tall as their mothers. It had been a great year for grass to grow.

As the fall came and the bull elk moved in the weather stayed warm and pleasant, the sun curing the grass into a golden tan color, the leaves turning golden and not falling from the trees. It was an Indian summer that seemed to late into the fall. Without a bitter snow storm to drive the elk and the little band of horse to the lower country they continued to graze on the tall grass from the summer staying in good shape. The only thing that changed was their winter coat they had grown and nice thick coat so if winter did come they were ready for it.

The weather stayed mild, with no bitter winds or harsh snow storms to drive them out most of the cow elk and the little band of horses remained in the basin. One day after getting a long drink from the stream that came from under a big rock, for no apparent reason the bay mare walked off in a direction that they had never been before.

She walked to the edge of the basin the opposite from where the cow elk liked to graze. They liked to graze more to the west side of the basin and the little band of horses usually grazed more the center on the southern side of the basin. The east side of the basin was covered in thick, loose rocks and grass, the rocks were not so easy for the animals to get around in. With the exception of the bull elk anytime something came into the basin or left, it was from the south side usually following one of the drainage's that left from the basin. The bull elk usually came in from the higher country to the northwest. The bay mare went to the east going further into the rocks than any of the horses had ever gone. This side was very rocky making the way slow the horses having to pick their way through the rocks until the bay mare came across an old trail the came into the basin from this side. The trail had not been used in a long time by anything other that an occasional deer or mountain lion making their way into the basin it was not a main thorough fare of any kind. With going easier on the trail the horses lined out single file behind the bay mare. The trail led them to the edge of the basin into some tall dark timber, then winding through many jagged boulders into a small rocky cut that took them down into a deep crater. The trail continued out the other side of the crater through a rough jagged cut, but the bay mare stopped in the bottom of the crater. The crater was maybe a half of a mile in diameter and in the very bottom was a small lake maybe six feet deep and two hundred yards across. Around the rim of the crater was shear rock bluff anywhere from a few feet high to over a hundred feet high. There were only two ways in or out of the crater, the one the horse had used coming in and the rough jagged cut that went out to the east side. The grass was tall and untouched and here the bay mare stopped dropped her head and began to graze. The little band of horses stayed in the crater for a few days before with the two brown mares and the two roan fillies behind her, the bay mare started back up the rough rocky trail that she had followed coming into the crater.

When the little band of horses came back into the basin the cow elk were all laying on the northern side of the basin taking in the sun's warmth. Most of the mature bull elk had drifted off to be alone or to join other bull elk making little bunches of bachelor bulls. The cows were left with a few young bulls and the calves. Other than a few flurries and light snows the weather stayed mild for the rest of the winter. The cow elk, a few deer and the little band of horses spent the winter in the basin.

Other than a few cold windy days the winter had not been unbearable at all for the little band of horses, there were very few frost, the snows were light usually only staying on the ground a few days before melting off it had been a strange winter. It had been the complete opposite to the year before, as the days grew longer and warmer the grass became drier as spring approached it was as if it had never rained or snow he past year. There were no spring snow storms and no spring rains only the warm rays of the sun and a few warm breezes during the days. What few bits of green grass that came up usually along the water ways or where there had been a big snow drift the previous year was eating almost as soon as it made its way out of the ground. The mares had stayed in food condition all winter grazing on the sun cured grass, the two fillies had grown into nice size horses for their two year old year. They were almost as tall as their mothers, but not as thick and heavy, that would come later. The cow elk had wintered good as well now most of the calves were weaned and were running in bunches of their same age soon these little bunches would leave the basin venturing out into the world on their own. The cows would be starting the cycle over again and the would forget about the calves from the year before giving their whole attention the calves being born this year.

As spring rolled into summer the sky was clear and the sun was hot there had only been one light shower all spring and only a few morning had, had any dew what so ever. The tall grass from the year before had lost a lot of it's nutritional value, but since there was plenty of it everything continued to remain in good condition.

The summer sun was relentless at the high altitude without any clouds as filters, the little band of horses took to grazing in the early morning's and early evenings the rest of the day was spent deep in the darkest timber they could get into. The cow elk had become almost completely nocturnal staying in the dark timber much of the day, coming out early evening.

Finally the breeze began to blow and with it came some clouds only a few in the beginning but after a couple of days they began to build up mostly to the west and north. Late in the evenings distant thunder could be heard across the basin. In the night distance flashes of lightning could be seen on the horizon, in the wind the horses could smell the distant moisture, but no rain came into the basin. There were a couple of afternoons that the clouds covered the sky and the sun was blocked for a few hours and then they were gone. These kind of set ups were all that came to the basin the coarse, tall grass from the year before dry and brittle and of little value to the horses.

CHAPTER
Ten

It began shortly after mid day the wind began to pick up clouds began rolling in there was a tingle in the air and the horses could feel it. It wasn't long before the hair in their tails was standing out waving in the wind and sticking to their thighs. Some of the hair in their manes was standing up and waving around while the mane hair that stayed against their necks was snapping and sparking when the mane came into contact with their necks. The air was charged with electricity and it was making the horses nervous and uncomfortable. The few elk that were still in the basin were running around mewing to their calves and each other not knowing what to do. In the distance the thunder could be heard it sharp and constant and moving closer to the basin, as it did the static in the air became more intense with blue charges of electricity arcing across if and of the horses came into contact with another horse. The horses were snorting and moving around trying to find a place where they could get relief from all of the static.

When the first bolt of lightning struck it was deafening, it should the ground where the horses stood they couldn't take it any longer so they began to run across the basin mixing in and chasing the cow elk and their calves. The second strike took out the top of one of the gnarled lightning scarred pine trees blowing splinters and sparks everywhere.

As it hit the old tree a blue arc shot across into another tree about a hundred yards away the top exploding as it did so. The steep peak to the north was being struck was almost rapid succession, the mares unable to take it any longer ran head long to the far side of the basin the cow elk following close behind. The bay mare taking the lead she headed straight for the rocky trail leading to the crater, they could not leave the basin fast enough.

They went into the crater in a dead run going down the rocky trail rolling rocks as they went, when the got to the bottom they ran around the small lake in the bottom before coming to a stop looking back at the rim where the lightning was still popping hot. The horses stood with their side heaving from the run their necks and flanks covered in sweat their eyes were wide from fear and their nostrils flared followed by snorting and high pitched whistles. The cow elk and their calves along with several mule deer came running into the crater not to far behind the horses, they were all running and milling around, the adrenaline from the fear caused by the lightning storm would not let them settle down.

Even though the roiling black clouds came in with the lightning and thunder there was only a few drops of rain to go along with all of the turmoil. The wind was whipping around seemly coming from all different directions before deciding on coming out of the south west. Even though the wicked storm last less than an hour it had seemed to go on forever as the storm passed over the crater the lightning striking the rim on several occasions the horses and all of the other critters that had came down into the crater, remained in the crater. The storm finally moving off into the distance leaving the night and the crater quiet except for the rustling of the horses and the elk in the tall grass.

The next morning the crater was full of thick blue smoke, it burned their eyes and irritated their nostrils and throats. As the day wore on more elk and deer along with an array birds and small animals made their way into the crater. There was even a couple of bobcats hanging in the big rocks under the rim of the crater coyotes came and drank water then went to lay up under the big boulders near the bottom. The elk, deer and horses all mingled together grazing and going to the small lake for water, some of the elk went out into the letting the water come over their backs. The air grew thicker with smoke and ash almost all activity stopped because it was so difficult for any of them to breathe. For two days the smoke lay heavy in the crater and on the third day flames were jumping up on both side of the crater. The fire had reached the crater and was going around it on both side the orange flame eating away at the tall grass and the trees along the edges of the rim. On the fourth day the air began to clear out a bit be a big relief to all of the animals that had taken refuge in the crater.

After several days the grass began to play out in the crater all but the coarsest grasses had been eaten down to the ground. The little band of horses began to be restless and frustrated with all of the close neighbors that come to the crater. The bay mare headed for the rocky trail that lead out of the crater the rest of the band fell in behind single file up and out of the crater. When the horses reached the top of the rim and as they followed the rocky trail back to the basin all of the grass was gone the trees gone or blackened from the fire. The tall grass from the year before that had been in the basin was all gone, in it's place was nothing but black ash. Little whirlwinds coming by and picking up the black ash of the old grass and scattering it into the wind. The only thing that was still in place was the stream that came out from under the big rock, there the horses drank and stood looking around water dribbling from their lips, taking a deep breath and letting out little snorts. They wandered around looking for some grass to eat, but the entire basin was black, what had been the treeline with the thick dark timber where they always went for cover in bad storms or hot days was only a blackened skeleton of the trees that had been there. All of the deep carpet of pine needles and grass was gone left behind was black scorched earth and rocks, the charred trunk remains of the huge old trees that had given them shelter so many times stood like blackened sentinels pointing straight into the sky most of the limbs and needles were gone.

There was nothing left that was familiar to the horses they wandered around smelling the ground, stopping sniffing the air some of the big stumps were still smoldering and some of the tree's roots were smoldering under the surface of the ground causing the smoke to come out of holes in the ground. There was no grass to be found for the little band of horses. The horses seemed to be lost not knowing where they should go, finally the bay mare took to an old trail that they had used several times leaving out of the basin.

The little band of horses rattled around in the charred mountain for several days before coming to the rim of a canyon there they found a steep and rocky trail down into the deep canyon. The grass had been spared from the fire and the water that came out from under the big boulder with the twisted gnarled tree growing out of it was fresh and cold. The little band of horses drank deep and then they began to eat their fill of the fresh grass they had eaten and drank very little since they had left the crater. Their sides were gaunt, their flanks drawn up, they were tired and sore footed from traveling on the rocky ridges that had once been covered with a soft carpet of pine needles now they were only covered with jagged rocks of all sizes. Without the canopy and shade from the big pines the sun blazed down on the backs of the little band of horses what had once been a pleasant place full of life and a place of refuge had become hot forbidden place with no life what so ever. Their heads and sides were covered with a black layer of charcoal from brushing against the charred trees that they had gone through on their way to the canyon with the rock rims. What little grass they had been able to find in along the way had been covered with fine ash they were hungry for the fresh grass that was in the canyon under the red rim rocks.

The little band of horses had been in the canyon for a few day when the sky began to darken as the clouds built up over the rim of the canyon, the wind began to pick up and the temperature began to drop all in a matter of minutes. The thunder could be heard in the distance coming closer with every rumble, soon there were some big drops of rain only a few at first then more came until it was a steady rain falling. The rain felt good to the horses it had been many months since they had felt the cleansing of the rain on their backs. The rain fell steady slowly washing the black char from their bodies it ran down their legs leaving black puddles on the ground around them. The rain continued for the rest of the afternoon leaving the canyon fresh with water dripping off of the trees and the grass heavy with the rain. The horses rolled and played bucking and rearing against each other for the first time in a long time. With their sides covered and their manes matted with the fresh mud the horses began grazing again. It was getting late in the season for green grass to have much of a chance, but if the weather didn't turn off completely cold it might have a shot. The next day started off hot and by midday the clouds had covered the sky over the canyon and the thunder was rumbling again soon the sky let loose of another round of life saving rain and again it last for most of the afternoon. By the next morning fresh shoots of green grass could been seen everywhere, he horses had there noses to the ground trying to get at everyone that they could get. The next few days were the same the mornings would be hot and the afternoons it would rain until late afternoon or even into the night. The new green grass had been held back for so long it seemed as if it was now working double time to catch up, it wasn't long until the canyon had a fresh green carpet of green grass.

   The horses had lost a lot of their weight and now they were eating almost all day and part of the night the new growth of grass was strong and soon the horses flanks were filled out and the hair was sleek and soft, their eyes were bright once again. Just as it had come to the canyon the rain stopped the sun came back out hot and with the recent rain the air was humid it felt good to horses their hides had been dry for so long. The one week of rain was all that came, for the rest of the summer it was hot days and cloudless skies. The grass grew quickly and began heading out in a short time it was not not as good had been in the past, but a lot better than it would have been if the rain had not come when it did.

The rains came into the basin at the same time it was raining in the canyon with the red rim rock, the parched ground soaked up every drop of rain that fell just like a big sponge. What ash was left from the fire went into the ground giving the soil nutrients that went straight into the grass. With the warm days the grass was growing rapidly trying to make seed before the early frost of the high elevation stopped all growth. The grass was able to reach a few inches in height before the early frost put a stop to anymore growth. The good thing is that the grass was able to grow tall enough to help hold the fragile top soil in place against erosion from the wind and rain. The fire had changed the basin and the whole mountain for that matter. It would be decades maybe centuries before there would ever be any timber in the basin again, for now there was just the charred skeletal remains of what had once been grand old pine trees. Much of the area around the basin that had only been rocks and timber was just a scorched wasteland now.

For the rest of the summer there wasn't anymore rains that made it on to the mountain or into the canyon with the red rim rocks. The clouds would come, the thunder in the distance could be heard and in the night there were even flashes of lightning to be seen against the horizon, but no rain. It seemed that by the time the rains made it across the wide valley to the west there just wasn't enough strength to make it onto the mountain. It seemed that the valley was receiving rain almost every time that it clouded up. All of this made no difference to the little band of horses, their only concern was the next bite of grass, their next drink of water and their safety from whatever elements might be lurking out there. Their needs were simple yet complex.

As the grass grew so did the two roan fillies they both were having a big surge of growth they were now every bit as tall as the mares and were beginning to fill out into thick muscular horses. Their once unblemished roan hides had darker patches of hair from when they may have gotten a cut or a scratch from a tree or a rock, or from a kick from one of the other horses that had scraped the hair off. As the hair grew back it was the dark blue color on the blue roan filly and it would be a dark reddish brown color on the bay roan filly. This was a nice looking set of horses that were running around the mountains unaware by anyone. Neither one of these two roan fillies having never seen a human nor felt the touch of one or had they ever experienced the confinement of a corral. They could become the first generation of long line of feral horses or they could be the last, their fate was yet to be determined.

As the summer came to an end so did the fresh green grass, the horses were all fat and in good physical shape. The days grew shorter and the grass quickly cured into a light golden color, the heads waving gently in the breezes that made their way down into the canyon. The oak brush along the canyon wall below the red rim rocks had turned to a crimson red, the mule deer that quietly stayed in the heavy brush were beginning to move around and bunching up. On occasion there would be two massive mule deer bucks doing battle shattering the stillness of the canyon with grunts, clattering horns and rolling rocks until finally one buck would turn and run defeated and exhausted. Having learned about the elk bulls when they were fighting the horses gave the mule deer a wide berth so as not to get caught up in their battles.

The days grew shorter and the nights grew much older, the mornings the frost would be heavy on the sun dried grass. The little band of horses were content with the canyon but the canyon was not big enough nor had it grown enough grass to accommodate the horses for the entire winter. So when the first big snow storm blew in and dropped several inches of snow most of the grass was covered up. The horses had to paw for every bite that they got. The first snow had settled and some of the grass was sticking out of the snow when the second snow storm came this one had much more snow and lasted several days. When the snow finally stopped and the sun came out the snow was almost knee deep to the horses. The horses continued to paw for their grass and the had been getting along good with deep snow and the covered grass. Everything was good until one day the sun was out and it was an unusually warm day causing the snow to condense and settle, that night the temperature dropped like a rock to a bone chilling cold. The next morning there was a thick crust beginning to form on the top of the snow making it harder for the horses to paw their way down to the grass that lay beneath the snow. The temperature continued to stay brutally cold the air a hazy blue color, sometimes early in the day there would be ice crystals floating in the air. The crust on the snow was getting thicker and harder for them to paw through. After a few days of pawing and moving around in the crust covered snow the hair on the front of the cannon bones on the horses lower legs began to be worn off making their legs sore and tinder. Little spots of blood could be seen on the ice that made the crust on the snow where the horses had stepped.

CHAPTER
Eleven

Early one bitter cold morning the bay mare made her way to the steep rocky trail that went up out of the canyon the rest of the mars followed her. The trail was covered in snow and slick but the little band of horses managed to scramble their way to the top once they had made there way to the top the going was much easier. The wind had reached the snow on the ridge and had swept much of it into drifts that they were able to make their way around. For several days the little band of horses moved across the steep foothills of the mountain grazing on the grass that the wind had blown the snow from eating snow to curb their thirst. The bay mare seemed to have a destination in mind but was a little unsure about it until one day the wind that came down out of the mountain was so strong and so cold that there became do doubt in her mind as to where they should go. With the wind roaring down upon them they made their way across several ridges and across several steep and slippery ravines until they came slipping into the wide valley with the creek coming down out of the mountain. The clouds of angry, black gnats had long since expired The wind had reached the valley floor and the snow lay in drifts around the rocks, trees and any other thing that stand up to the wind. Much of the grass bared off from the wind whipping across the valley floor. The water running open clear and cold, the little band of horses stopping to take on the first drink of water that they had, had for several days they stood near the stream drinking and standing then drinking some more until their thirst had been satisfied for the time being. Then they began to graze on the open, sun cured grass.

Soon the bay mare and the two brown mares began to pick up on something that was very strange to them, they had come upon tracks and sign of other horses. They stopped their eating and dropped their heads and were snorting and sniffing the ground walking following the tracks. Other than the old roan stallion they had never encountered any other horses the whole time that they had been rambling around the mountain and now they had come on to fresh sign of other horses in the area. After investigating the fresh horse sign for a few minutes their hunger took over and they went back to grazing on the golden grass, they lost interest in the other horses, for the time being anyway. There was also some elk in the wide little valley, but not near as many as had been there when the horses spent the winter here before. After the big fire most of the elk migrated to the north up the chain into fresh country beyond the scorched path the fire had left. It would be several years before the elk in any numbers would make their return. Many of the elk in the wide little valley were in poor condition after spending the summer looking for decent grass after the big fire, and when the Arctic like temperature moved in it was more than several of them could endure. Their carcasses littered the wide little valley with the coyotes, magpies and ravens arguing over the remains and putting up loud protests when one or the other was forced away. A few raised their heads and looked at the little band of horses as they entered the valley and began to graze, but for the most part the elk paid little attention to the horses as they began their grazing.

The little band of horses were so intent on their grazing that they failed to notice the other horses when they came into view, it wasn't until they heard a loud whistle and snort that their heads came up and the became aware of the strange horses. The five horses all looking in the direction that the loud whistle had come from, there stood two horses their heads high their nostrils flared and their tails standing straight out one was sorrel with a streak face and the other was a bay with a streak face and three white socks. Sorrel had what was left of a halter around his neck with a frayed short piece of rope what had been the lead rope hanging from the halter. Apparently the bay had broken or lost his halter if he had ever had one at all. These two strange horses were both geldings and they had gotten a way from someone before wondering into the little wide valley with the creek coming out of the mountain.

The five mares all moved at once as the ran to the two geldings their heads held high and their tails standing straight out the five mares surrounded the two geldings touching noses snorting and squealing as they crowded around then with ears laid back wheeling around and kicking the geldings landing solid thumps with both hind legs on the gelding ribs and bellies. The geldings turning and kicking with their hind feet just the same after a lot of kicking, squealing, snorting, and pawing at each other they all took of in a race around the little valley the mares biting and kick out at the geldings as they ran. After the introduction with geldings the mares went back to grazing and the gelding keeping a safe distance from them as they to went back to grazing. Almost as if nothing had ever happened. For several days the horses grazed together yet separate from each other, every time one of the gelding would get to close one or more of the mares would rush him with ears pinned back teeth bared biting big clumps of hair from the hides of the geldings if they got close enough. Gradually the mares loosened their vigilant control and let the geldings into their tight little band.

The winter stayed bitter cold with very little more snow even the bright sun shine couldn't penetrate the blue cold air that had settled in the little wide valley. By the time that the icy hands of winter started to loosen their grips it was already into early spring the grass in the little wide valley was played out the elk had moved off to find a better place to find food several found their way on to the hay meadows down below and into the hay stacks put up the summer before for winter feed for the cattle. The horses stayed on in the valley eating the dry leaves and small branches of the brush that grew along the foot o the ridge above the valley.

By the time spring finally fought it's way into the little wide valley the horses were thin their long thick winter coats dull they were tired it had been a long hard winter. The few inches of lead rope left that was attached to halter hanging around the sorrel gelding's neck has turned into a ball of ice from being dipped into the cold stream water ever time the gelding put his head down and took a drink. The ice ball thumped the gelding chest and arms every time he moved around being awkward and irritating to the gelding. With the coming of spring this time instead of rain showers or snow flurries there came the wind at first it was a cold wind but as the days moved along it began to warm up taking the frost from the frozen ground and softening it up. Early one particularly windy day the bay mare headed for the head of the wide little valley the two brown mares and the two roan mares falling in behind her, the two geldings standing on as they moved away. The geldings nickering to the mares but they continued on there way, the mares started up the incline on the trail that led out of the valley before the two gelding broke loose and galloped to catch up to the little band of horses. As the horses moved back into the burned mountain they were able to take advantage of the small grassy parks that came across with the snow still drifted in the shade they were able to eat enough snow to keep them going. When they came across a small park the horses would drop their heads and graze until the grass was all gone it tasted good after eating leaves and branches. When they happened on to any small streams they would stand around and drink and drink some more until they couldn't hold any more water before they would move on looking for the next grassy park. Even though the burn had striped the mountain of most of it's tree cover they managed to find little parks that were mostly out of the wind. The days gradually began to warm up and the wind relaxed as the days grew longer the band of horses looking thinner and shaggier than ever before finally walked out into the basin. The air was cold and the short grass from the summer before waving gently in the wind, the band of horses walked to the stream that came out from under a big rock and drank the cold clear water, their first drink in several days. With all of the trees in the timberline gone from the fire, the only place they could find to get out of the sharp wind was behind the big boulders that lay around the upper part of the basin. There they found warm places out of the wind and rested, some of them standing with their heads down and a hind leg cocked, the rest laying down flat on their sides trying to soak up as much of the sun's warmth that they could. It had been a long, cold, hard winter and they were tired.

CHAPTER
Twelve

Slowly the days got warmer and the band of horses grazed on last years grass in the basin, many days spending the warmer part of the lounging on the sunny side of the big boulders letting the sun drive the deep cold from the hard winter and the night before out of their bones. It had been the hardest winter that three mares had endured since they had been forced into the mountains, it had taken it's toll on them the scarce grass and spells with no water had drained the energy and the flesh from their bodies. The biter cold had penetrated them to the core and it was going to take a lot of sunshine and green grass to put them back on track. The grass from the summer before was short and dry and had lost most of it's nutritional value, it was keep their bellies full but it wasn't giving them a lot of energy or strength. It would keep them going till the rains came and the grass turned green again and finally the rains did come to the basin. It was way up in the summer before the first good rain came to the basin the dry parched earth soaking up ever drop like the big sponge that it had become. The horses still patchy with patches of winter hair that was still in place and had not yet turned loose, were a site not to easy on the eyes. Compared to how they usually looked this time of year all fat and slick and shiny they looked rough, after the first good rain they had all rolled in the fresh mud, the mud sticking to the dead winter hair in matted clumps making the already coarse looking horses look even worse.

After the rain it was almost over night the grass began to grow and green up it had been laying in wait of the much need moisture before making it's first appearance of the year. With new growth of green grass came a few of the cow elk that usually spent the summer in the basin, this summer however there were only a few compared to what had usually summered there in the past. After the big fire most of the big herds of elk had moved further north deeper into the mountains finding new country and mixing in with other herds, the basin was like a ghost town. The cow elk that came into the basin this time had, had as hard of a winter as the horses had, they thin and shaggy with very few calves the winter had been difficult for them as well. Many of the elk winter-killed thinning the herds down even more. It really didn't matter to the horses if the elk were there or not they just wanted the green grass and warm sunshine. Slowly the horse began to put on weight and the dry dead winter hair found it's way to the ground, the horses slicked off but a long ways from having the fat that they would need to get through another winter like the last one. Other rains came and the grass doing it's best after such a late start to finish off by first frost. The band of horses were doing their best to make that deadline too, it was eat, drink, snooze, soak up some sun, eat some more go get another drink.

The rains that came into the basin this summer were extremely violent the lightning striking numerous charred skeleton trees that remained standing along the edge of the basin causing them to explode sending splinters and pieces of debris in every direction. On more than one occasion the horses retreated to the crater during these violent storms it had become their safe place to go when things became to uncomfortable in the basin. It was on one of these runs to the crater that the sorrel gelding caught what was left of the halter that was hanging around his neck on a burnt snag, the snag still solid and tempered from the fire, held as the halter held briefly before breaking the rotten halter spinning the gelding around because the gelding was going so fast after it sun him around he lost his balance flipping over backwards and rolling two times before he regained his feet dazed and confused, running nickering catching up to the other horses. The grass in the crater was good and fresh but the lake had dried up so it was no longer a place that they could stay for any length of time before needing to come out for a drink of water. Whether because of the big fire or because of other circumstances or a combination of several things the mountain had become harsh less inviting place to try and make an existence. With the tree cover gone and exposing the bare charred rocky ground the summer sun beat down relentlessly making the already dry mountain drier. Even though the grass did it's best the early frost stopped it in it's tracks shutting everything down for another year, maybe next year would be better. It had been a dry summer for the basin and for the mountain and it had been an even drier summer for the lower country and the country down below out in the plains. Since the big fire the rains had changed how they came across this part of the mountain, for the valleys to the west the rains had come early and stayed late the weather mild and pleasant. The rains taking the path to the north of the mountain going north and east from there, the mountain and the country to the south and east getting very little rain and a lot of wind. The rains that did make it into these areas were fast and violent leaving very little rain in it's path.

 When the cold winds of autumn began to blow there were no golden leaves scattering on the ground in the basin this fall, the horses had regained most of their weight and condition, their winter coats of hair thick and long, they would be ok once they got into the lower country and if the winter wasn't a repeat of the previous one. The wind blew cold but the band of horses hung onto their place in the basin it was if they were hoping it was only a false alarm and the sun would be warm and the grass would turn green again. The summer had been a short one up in the high country and it was looking like it was going to be another long dry cold winter. The band of horses grazed with their tails to wind, resting behind the big boulders on leeward side, they stayed until the wind turn into a bitter cold hearted beast that they could not endure any longer. The bay mare taking her place in the lead the rest of the band of horses following her, with wind blowing cold and strong on their tails they started making their way down out of the basin.

The band of horses rambled around the charred burn scars finding grass but always on the hunt for water, since there had been no snow the only water was small springs and little mountain streams, but many of them no longer had water running the full length. Some just had small frozen over pools that the horses had to paw through the ice to get a much needed drink. Others what had been good springs were reduced to mere seeps the band of horses standing pawing at these small seeps waiting for enough water to take a sip sometimes they stood around all night before they all were able to get enough water to move on. Finally the bay mare led them to the canyon with red rim rock with water coming out from under the big boulder with twisted little pine tree growing out of it. As the made their way down steep and rocky trail they got the sense that something had changed, something wasn't right when they reached the bottom the was strange kind of smell that they had never experienced before the whole canyon was covered in this smell and the grass that had always covered the canyon floor gone it had been grazed and trampled to the ground only a few coarse dry weeds remained. The band of horses walked around sniffing the ground with low snorts finally going to the spring and getting a big drink of the fresh water that came from under the big boulder. Other than the drink the trip had not been very fruitful.

With the conditions being so dry and grass being so scarce during the summer the ranchers had pushed their herds further into the mountain than they been in several decades, here in the canyon with the red rim rocks they had filled it with a band of sheep holding them there until every blade of grass had been eaten before moving them to a different location or taking them down lower country to be fed hay or put on trucks and shipped to a place with better feed.

The band of horses stood around the spring most of the night drinking their fill of the fresh sweet water before making the steep climb up the rocky trail. Once on top of the rim rock the horses began grazing on the coarse bunch grass the covered most of the ridge. For several days the band of horses would spend one or two days grazing the ridges and then making their way back down the steep rocky trail they would spend the night drinking from the spring that came out from under the big boulder with the twisted tree growing in it. With their thirst satisfied they would make the climb back up the steep rocky trail where they would begin their search for grass all over again. As the days grew shorter and shorter and the winds grew colder the grass grew more scarce forcing the band of horse to forage further up into the cold, windy ridges. The horses spending more and more time looking for grass, sometimes not going down for water but every three or four days. They soon began to lose the weight that they had been able to accumulate during the summer their ribs began to show through the long thick winter coat.

The wind was exceptionally cold and strong and the grass had become very scarce when the bay mare raised her head and took the lead quartering into the wind her head bent shielding it from the wind the best she could the rest of the band of horses soon following her their place in line. For two days she led her little band across steep and frozen ravines, over wind ravaged slopes and rocky rims that would have made the cow elk envious, before coming into the wide little valley with the stream of fresh cold water coming out of the mountain. What had once been a strong mountain stream was now just a small trickle compared to what it had been frozen solid in many places and the grass that had covered the floor of the wide little valley, like the floor of the canyon with the red rim rocks, was gone the was no grass left the floor instead was covered with dry and frozen cow pies the grass grazed and trampled to the ground. The story much the same as the canyon with the red rim rocks only the cattle ranchers had been forced to push their cattle up into the higher valleys and hanging on as long as they possibly could before moving their cattle to lower pastures or meadows hoping for a mild winter and a better year next year. With the stream being so weak and frozen the band of horses had a hard time finding a pool with enough water for them to drink.

The band of horse stood around their pool most of the night pawing at the ice and drinking the water as it came into the pocket they had created. They were hungry, cold, tired and sore footed from their march across the foothills, with the dawn of morning came a bitter change in the temperature the horses breath causing frost and ice to accumulate around their nostrils and around their face ears and eyes. The frost settling on their manes along their backs and on the heads of their tails. The bay mare took the lead back up the head of the valley into the steep ridges the drained into the wide little valley there they went after the coarse frosty grass that grew along the slopes. With the drop in the temperatures came the snow at first it was just a few flakes later the skies becoming much darker the snow began to fall in heavier amounts, lasting for the rest of the day and into the following morning. By the time the snow had come to a stop it had dropped well over a foot of powdery snow, covering all of the available grass left on the mountain. For the band of horses the job of getting their bellies full had just doubled in terms of difficulty, now they had to paw through the snow before they could even get a bite of the tough dry coarse grass. Between the added difficulty of getting to the grass and finding frozen pools of water that they could paw through the ice in order to get a drink coupled with the now bitter cold the physical condition of the band of horse began to drop off sharply.

The horses were only barely holding their own against the mountain when the bitter cold wind came rushing out of the north. The powdery snow had been laying on the ground for over two weeks when the wind hit, because of the extreme cold the snow had only settled a very small amount and it had remained loose and powdery. As the strength of the wind increased it began picking up the snow from the ground causing a blinding ground blizzard, looking straight up the sky was clear blue and the sun was shining, but on the surface of the mountain it was an entirely different view. The band of horses had foraged their way much further up into the steep slopes looking for grass when the wind hit driving them off of the ridge and into a small ravine to get away from as much of the harsh blast of the wind that they could. The wind packing their tails full of the driving snow and plastering long thick winter hair of their rumps and back legs with the white stuff, the hard wind soon had the ridges completely bared off exposing the coarse dry grass the snow piling up behind anywhere the wind could be blocked many drifts ten to twelve feet high packed hard by the force of the wind. The wind had been raging for over two days forcing the band of horses to stay put in their little bit of a wind break ravine. The long thick winter coat on all of the horses was completely packed and matted with snow from the wind they were a ghostly white with the only thing showing that they were even alive were their eyes. Their big dark round eyes were like black diamonds in the snow. They had all been standing with their heads down tails against the wind, when the bay mare raised her head up and looked around, the two brown mares did like wise. Soon the bay mare looking more like some kind of snow creature moved off taking the lead the rest of the band of horses falling in behind her looking like a group of moving snow creatures. The wind not showing any signs of giving up any of it power continued to batter the horses as they made their way across the slopes, making good time crossing the wind swept bare ridges taking much more time working through and across the drifted snow. Sometimes they could find a way around the drifts, sometimes the snow was packed so hard that they could merely walk over it and sometimes they fell through floundering to the other side using up a lot of strength and energy. By night fall the horses had found a deep ravine with good amount of exposed grass that was mostly out of the wind. The two days standing against the wind in the little ravine up on the slope and the days march of going through the snowdrifts had left the horses give out and hungry.

As the wind roared through the night the horses took advantage of the grassy area that they had come into grazing and resting through out the night. As the dawn began to break the bay mare once again taking the lead stepped out into the storm the rest of the horses close behind. For most of the day the band of horse fought their way across the mountain against the fierce bitter wind, slowly making their way over, around, or through the newly drifted snow. By late afternoon the band of horses came to an out of the wind place with a little bit of grass for them to eat, trembling with exhaustion the horses soon had all of the grass consumed and were browsing on some of the nearby bushes, eating and licking the packed snow their bodies were craving a drink of water. The band of horses rested through the night staying out of the wind as much as they could come morning they were on the move once again. They had been working their way down the mountain at the same time as they were moving across it, slowly getting them into lower country. Luck was on the side of the band of horse on afternoon of the third day they stumbled into a small stream covered in a layer of snow the horses fell through trying to cross the bottom of the ravine. The horses spent the rest of the day and most of the night satisfying their compounded thirst. On the fourth day the horses made it into lower country they had left most of the cold bitter wind behind up on the higher slopes of the mountain, after having their fill of fresh water the night before the horses were in a little better shape the hungry, sore footed and tired, but feeling better with their bellies full of water. Late on the fourth day they came crossed over a divide into completely different territory than they had ever been before, yet it felt familiar to the three older mares, after crossing over the divide they came across a grassy slope out of the wind here they settled in and began grazing like the exhausted hungry horses that they were. Although it was still the dead of winter with some of the harshest weather still coming when they crossed over that divide it was like they had moved into a completely different Eco System the wind died down and the temperature was much warmer and as they got further from the angry mountain it improved even more. By the time they reached the bottom it was as if they had walked through a door from winter into spring. The moon was full and the horses exhausted yet there was a burning need for the bay mare to be off of the mountain. After a few hours of grazing the bay mare moved out into the moonlight the rest of the band of horses close behind they traveled through the night making their way down into a valley that long ago had been home to them. With the breaking of the dawn on the fifth day the little band of horses moved out on to the valley floor, the valley floor covered with tall untouched grass. A little further in was a nice stream of cold fresh water flowing the length of the valley, the stream flowed in the bottom of a deep and sometimes wide draw with slopes that were steep yet accessible. The band of horses fell in line behind the bay mare following an old cow trail that led them down into the creek bottom into a grove of huge old cottonwood trees, here they stopped and drank their fill of the fresh cold water and then they dropped their heads and went to grazing. The little band of horses were hungry, exhausted, sore footed, but content with the place that they had found.

After drinking their fill from the stream the horses began grazing along the creek bank along with the tall dry grass was fresh green grass that had just begun to grow mixed in with older grass. The tinder blades of green tasted good to the horses and they grazed their hunger away for the time being anyway, as the sun came out and as it moved higher into the sky it spread its warmth across the creek bottom. With their bellies full of fresh grass and their thirst taken care of, their bodies exhausted from the march across the mountain into the valley they let themselves be consumed by the warmth and soon they were all stretched out in the deep carpet of warm dry leaves sound a sleep.

The horses slept past midday into the early afternoon, the sun was starting to make it's way across the western sky when the horses started to wake up and stir around. As they would set up they would lay back down and make attempts a rolling rubbing their heads on the ground doing a lot of groaning they finally gave up and got up walked to the stream got another long drink of the cold fresh water, then they went back to grazing once again. The band of horses continued to graze through the rest of the afternoon into the early twilight hours of the evening before resting again. Every day was about the same for the band of horses, graze on the tall fresh grass, drink the cold fresh water from the creek sleep through the warmest part of the day. There had been one afternoon that bay mare had sensed an intruder she had raised her head and tested the air looking over her back and all around for any sighs of danger, after not being able to detect any she went back to grazing.

For the short time that the band of horses had been in the valley along the creek bottom the weather had been unseasonably warm, compared to the bitter snow filled wind that had pushed them out of the mountains it was like summer in the basin. During the day while the horses were grazing their necks, flanks, and wrinkles above their eyes and around their ears would be wet with sweat. The warmth had felt good to their bodies driving out the penetrating cold that they had brought with them from the mountain. One afternoon there came a sharp rush of much cooler wind and the sky began filling up with clouds, by nightfall the sky was completely overcast and a colder wind had began to blow, soon the air was filled with big wet snowflakes covering the backs of the horses as they made their way into the grove of cottonwood trees there they turned the tails against the wind and rested as the storm slammed it's way across the valley.

CHAPTER
Thirteen

The snow storm continued to pack the screen to the window to Samantha's room and the last time she tried to look out the window all she saw was screen full of packed wet snow. She could here the snow flakes hitting against the house on the outside, it was very hard for her concentrate on doing her school she was so worried about the band of horses and the storm that was raging outside her window. When it finally came time for her to go to bed she had a hard time falling asleep she was tossing around so much, she never new when she fell asleep when she woke up she could still here the wind howling outside and the Grey, light of a snowy morning had filled her room. She got up quickly and tried to look out her window but the packed snow prevented that she got dressed quickly and made her way downstairs, there her father was setting at the table with a cup of coffee and her mother was just pulling some biscuits out of the oven and they smelled delicious, that was when she realized that she was very hungry. They had the radio in that set in the window over the sink turned on and the woman's voice that was coming out of it was calling for a "Stock man's Advisory" and it was to be in affect until further notice, she went on to say that the storm that was raging outside was estimated to drop between two and three feet of snow depending on elevation. Because of the late season of the storm there were a lot of baby calves and lambs that had already been born earlier in the spring, the storm was shaping up to be what they called a calf-killer. That was where the calves were laying down out of the storm and the snow would cover them up suffocating them where they lay. Samantha was worried about the horses but there was nothing she could do.

Since just about every road was closed and people were being advised not to get out in the storm after breakfast the girl and her mom and dad decided how they should spend their day, it had been a long time since the three of them had any opportunity to be together as a family. For the morning they decide they should play board games finish off the afternoon with a card game maybe Cribbage then they would have a good dinner, then everyone could go their own way for the rest of the evening. As the family kept the fire going and played their games the storm showed no signs of weakening, the valley had not seen the likes of such a storm for several decades. All day long the girl thought about the horses realizing that they had experienced much worse and had always managed to come through, at least they had, had a few days of nice weather and had been able to get their bellies full of the new grass before this storm hit, that would make a lot of difference right there.

As the day wore on there was lots of laughter and good natured kidding around the game table, they had set down and had their evening meal then they all sort of drifted to their own spaces, Samantha making her way up to her room, her dad reading a book by the fire and her mom doing things in the kitchen that she had thought about during the day. Once up to her room Samantha's thoughts were filled with the thoughts of the horses and how they were getting along, from the way it was looking it might be several days before she could even make her way down to the creek. Samantha way trying to concentrate on reading her book when she set up and put the book down, she had completely forgot that she had received a pair of cross-country shies for Christmas last year but because there had never been enough snow to try them out they had got pushed to the very back of her closet. She was in her closet digging and rearranging things until she was able to drag out the skies, the boots had been way to big back then so hopefully she hadn't out grown them by now. She shoved her foot down into the boots they were still to big but with a heavy pair of socks she was pretty sure she was in business.

The storm was still blowing strong when the girl finally went to bed, and like the night before sleep did not come quickly, she lay awake thinking about her skies and how well she would be able to use them. She was also worried about the horses and where they had spent the day had they found a good place out of the wind or had they gotten caught out in the open and had to endure the full force of the storm? Sometime after she had fallen asleep the storm began to relax and blow itself out, when the morning arrived and the cold Grey snow light had penetrated her room she woke up to an eerie stillness, there was no wind howling and the house was completely silent ever noise muffled by the snow that covered almost everything. Samantha woke up thinking about her plan to cross-country sky to the creek, she hoped it would work. The storm had passed but the sky was still heavy overcast and it appeared much darker than it actually was.

Samantha got up and quickly got dressed and went down the stairs to find her mom and dad already up and having coffee, she looked outside and realized that her plan might not be the right plan for right now. The snow around the big barn was drifted up past the eves of the roof some twenty feet up and out into the big pole pen, the front of the shop was not visible because of the drift that reached all the way to the peak of the roof. The chicken house was under a mound of deep snow. The ground was bare around her dads truck but her moms car was somewhere under a huge snow drift. It looked like the day was going to to be spent just digging out. Samantha sat at the table with her dad while her mother made a tasty breakfast of pancakes, eggs and bacon. They were going to need all the energy that they could get before the day was over. The first order was to get the chicken house dug out so that they could take care of their chickens.

For two days the sky stayed dark under heavy clouds, the little family doing their best to make paths and uncover all the things that they needed it was hard daunting work requiring numerous breaks and new plans made. On the morning the third day the sun made it's appearance for the first time in several days it was a welcome site and as it was burning it's way through the clouds they started hearing a noise it was a ways down the road, it was the county working it's way up the road pushing the snow off either side. Soon after lunch time the big yellow maintainer burst it's way into the yard making a pass opening up the driveway, the driver stopped and talked to her dad for a couple of minutes then he was gone again, it was a welcome site.

They had been so busy trying to clear paths and uncover things from the snow that she had hardly had time to think about the horses and at night she was to tired to think about them she had fallen asleep as soon as her head touched the pillow. By the fifth day the sun had regained most of it's strength and was doing it's best to be rid of the snow, the snow was melting and settling and the mud was taking the place of bared ground. At night it would freeze up and by mid morning the water would be dripping and puddles growing bigger everyday. Her dad would leave early in the morning while the roads were frozen and not return until late after it had set up good after dark. It had been fun not to have to go to school for those two days but after the road was plowed out the vacation was over. Because the road was so bad during the day Samantha would ride into town with here dad and wait at his office until time for school then she would walk out to the school, after school she would go to his office and wait until they could make it back into their house. Her mom stayed home by herself and she would have supper ready for the hungry two when they got in. They had settled into a new routine adjusting to the new snowy conditions.

Away from the buildings the snow had less resistance baring off the ridges and filling in the draws and low spots with the white stuff, The tall grass had stopped most of it and the snow was knee deep all the way to really deep in some of the deeper draws. The sun had settled the heavy snow and the cold temperatures at night would freeze it at night making a thick hard crust on top of the snow. The ground underneath the snow still warm and soaking up all the moisture that it could. By the end of the week with the exception of the big drifts and what was in the shady places most of the snow was gone and most of the mud was drying up as well. Samantha had been disappointed that she still hadn't gotten to use her cross-country skies, sometimes things just don't work out as planned, maybe next year. There had been a lot of snow, but it wasn't very good for that kind of skiing. She was looking forward to the weekend so she could go look for the horses she it had been over a week since she had seen them, the weekend couldn't get here soon enough.

CHAPTER
Fourteen

By the time Friday afternoon got there Samantha was almost shaking with anticipation the warm sun had gained the upper hand and the snow retreated to just the drifts, the ground had taken in all the moisture and it was beginning to dry out on the surface. The afternoons were starting to be longer having more daylight after they had gotten home. After supper and getting the dishes cleaned up Samantha went upstairs to her room and there she plotted out what she thought she could do the next morning, she was thinking that she might even make her a sandwich, yes that was probably a good idea.

It had taken her a long time to finally fall asleep she was so excited about going and looking for the band of horses the next morning. The Grey light of dawn had replaced the darkness of the night in her room when she woke up, she climbed out of bed got dressed and went down stairs to the kitchen where her mom had just finished putting some biscuits into the oven, it looked like they were having biscuits and gravy this morning, her mom always knew what to make for breakfast. After she had biscuits and gravy she had one with just butter and apple jelly, then she helped her mother with the dishes she did take time out to grab a biscuit and stuff a piece of sausage in the middle of it, stick it in a plastic bag and stuck that in her pocket then out the door she went heading for the creek in the lower pasture. The ground was fluffy after all of the snow, and it had been dried out by the sun and the wind as she walked the ground was soft and she left deep foot prints in the fresh soil.

When Samantha got to the creek the first place she went was to the grove of big cottonwoods, there was still a lot snow drifted in the bottom of the creek bottom, the creek itself was running bigger than she had every seen it run in some places the banks were full and in other places the water was out of the banks and flowing across the creek bottom. She found where the horses has spent at least part of the storm the area was stomped out and then it had filled back in with fresh snow after the horses had moved away. She followed the snow filled tracks down the creek a ways and there she found where the horses had spend the remainder of the storm as well as a few days afterwards. There had been a thick patch of willows in a bend in the creek here is where the horses had stayed, the willows had been eaten down level with the snow the deep snow having covered all of the grass the horses had turned to willows for something to eat. The willow patch was gone but, horse tracks and piles of sign were everywhere but no horses they had left as soon as the snow settled enough for them to go in search of fresh grass. Samantha could not get over the fact that the horses had eaten the whole willow patch. The girl kept following the tracks and the sign down the creek she had no idea that horses moved around so much when they were looking for food. The tracks crossed and zig-zagged and recrossed the creek dozens of times, it was well into the morning before she came to a trail with fresh looking tracks going out of the creek bottom, Samantha had found a dead tree that had fallen across the creek and she was able to crawl across the tree and get to the other side of the creek, she followed this trail for what seemed like a long ways before she finally saw the horses off in the distance out on a grassy flat.

Samantha had not anticipated the horses being so far from the creek and she had not anticipated that the creek bottom would still be so full of snow and she hadn't thought about the creek being so full with the run off, she was learning lots of life's lessons even if she hadn't caught up to the horses. After she spotted the horses she walked toward them for a ways before realizing that they were a lot further than they looked out on that flat. The sun was high overhead and she was a long was from home, she sat down on a rock pulled her biscuit out of her pocket and ate it all the while trying to decide what she should do. Finally she stood up put the plastic bag in her pocket and headed back to the dead tree that was laying across the creek. After crawling back across the creek on the dead tree she started working her way back up the creek to the grove of big cottonwoods from there taking her cow trail that led towards her house. She had been gone a long time and by the time she walked into her yard she had, had enough and she was tired, walking in the deep snow and mud had made for a long day. She did her evening chores and then she went inside and up up to her room, after supper and after the dishes were done she took her shower and went to bed, she was asleep as soon as her head touched her pillow.

The next day Samantha's plans got changed her mother had some household chores for her to do, starting with cleaning her room, it had been a while since it had, had a floor to ceiling cleaning and it looked like today was going to be the day for that. The sun was warm and the there was not a breath of wind it was a perfect early spring day, the massive snow drifts that were around the barn and shop were still a long way from disappearing they were slowly melting and the dark mud that was beneath them made it a messy task to get very close to them. Her and her mom cleaned on the upstairs, her focusing on her room, they worked steady until around noon that was when her mother suggested that they take a break and have some lunch. They were setting at the table when her dad came in he had went down to the lower end of the valley to get some papers signed by a rancher down that way and he was back. As he set down to join them he mentioned the rancher had mentioned that he had seen a little band of horses along the creek down that way. When he tried to get close to them they had taken off back up the creek this way. Samantha felt her breath suck in, what did this rancher think about the horses? And was he going to ignore them or was he thinking something should be done? When she ask all her dad said was that the man figured that they belonged to some ranch on the other side of the big range from out on the flats somewhere. Maybe they had been caught in the storm and had drifted into this valley. No one seemed overly concerned about the horses especially her dad it had only been a topic for conversation for him, the lasted gossip.

The next day was a school day but spring break would be starting this coming Friday Samantha was hoping that she could last that long before going to look for the horses. Maybe if there was a good afternoon in there she could go look around down at the creek, maybe the snow would be gone from the creek bottom by then her last trip had not been very fruitful as far as getting close o the horses went. All to soon they were back up stairs this time they were putting things away and by chore time they had pretty well wrapped up their day of cleaning.

The week went a lot faster than Samantha had thought it was going to go, she made it to Friday the ride home on the bus seemed to take the longest. When the bus finally pulled to her stop Samantha got off let out a big sigh of relief and walked to the house, her mother was standing near the stove stirring a pan of chocolate pudding when she ask her mother why she had made pudding she simply said "because it's spring break. Want some?" The pudding was much better than she remembered it being and soon they had made a big dent in it there was barely enough for her dad when he got home. She had been making plans all week and now the break was here she was hoping that things would go good for her this time. It had been a long time since she had seen the horses up close.

CHAPTER
Fifteen

The next morning Samantha was up early got dressed and went downstairs, her dad was setting at his place drinking coffee with her mom she sat down and joined them when her mom ask her what kind of plans she had for spring break, she thoughtfully replied that she wanted to try to find the horses that everyone had heard about. Her mom raised her eyebrows and her dad grinned behind his coffee cup, she had thought that this was the best way to move the horses into their conversations since they were no longer a secret. After breakfast her mom told her to come with her down to the barn, curious she followed along behind mother to the barn. Once in the barn her mother went back to what had been the feed room there on the floor were two white square blocks covered with a very fine dust her mother brushed away the dust and with a hammer that she brought with her gave the corner of the block a solid blow with the hammer two more wacks came and then a wedge shaped corner broke off onto the floor, the chunk of salt was about six inches long and four inches wide and a couple of inches thick. The girl curious ask her mother what purpose of a chunk of salt this size. She told her that if she ever got close enough for the horses to smell her they would smell the salt and they might forget that she was a person, maybe letting them become friendly with her.

Samantha thought it was worth a shot so she put the piece of salt in her little back pack next to her sandwich and she was off for the grove of big cottonwoods down at the creek bottom.

    For no bigger than it was the little chunk of salt was heavy and it got heavier as she made her way down to the creek bottom. When she reached the grove of big cottonwoods she was a little disappointed that there were not any horses there, the snow was gone and the fresh dark green grass was several inches tall it looked like there had not been anything here since the snow storm all of the sign that she found was old and dry. The creek was still running back to back the snow melt was going on further up into the mountains were the creek began, keeping it full for sometime yet to come. She worked way down the creek always looking for fresh sign or tracks moving slow and keeping an eye on the horizon just in case. She went to the tree that lay across the creek and crawled across to the other side from there she made her way up out of the creek bottom to where she had last seen the horses way off in the distance. She stood and looked in all directions for several minutes nothing that could be considered a group of horses could be seen. Slowly she made her way back down into the creek bottom, back over the tree that was laying across the creek and up to the grove of big cottonwoods. The trees were just starting to leaf out and they had a green color to their tops, she had never seen the grass so green underneath the big trees.

    She made her way to an old tree trunk that was laying on its side there she took off her pack and set it beside her and took out her sandwich and slowly ate it as she was thinking about a new plan, that was when she saw them, they were slowly grazing their way up the creek, and they were moving into the area around the grove of trees. She had just stuck the plastic bag that her sandwich was in back inside of her backpack and it was setting on the tree trunk next to her she sat very still, afraid that if she made any kind of move at all that they would run away, and she would never see them again. She could not believe her luck she sat there not moving just barely breathing, the horses not paying her any mind whatsoever kept grazing almost coming straight toward her. The horses were just a few feet away when the bay with the streak face raised his head and softly snorted, he was almost close enough for her to reach out and touch, but she remained still her heart beating so fast that she thought that it was going to burst. The bay horse stood there in mid chew grass hanging out of the side of his mouth looking at her not moving not even blinking an eye. Finally, after what seemed like hours the bay horse reached out his nose and sniffed in her direction. Still, she didn't make any move by now the other horses had picked up on the bay horse's curiosity and were gathering around the two roan mares were acting the most nervous of them all, the girl did not realize that this was the first time that either of them had ever seen a human and it had been many years since the three older mares had seen a human. The streak faced bay was both curious and friendly he had grown up around humans and they always had some kind of a treat he was working his sense of smell hoping that there was some kind of a treat here with this one. Slowly he made his way up to the girl reaching as far as he could reach with his nose and he took a sniff of her knee on his first attempt to smell the girl he flinched scaring himself causing himself to jump a little bit, Samantha almost jumped herself she had no idea why she hadn't. Soon the bay horse was back smelling at the girls knee and sniffing at her jacket near her shoulder then he was smelling and blowing his soft muzzle gently brushing against her face, she sat there afraid that the sound of her beating heart was going to scare them all away. As the streak faced bay horse kept working his nostrils over Samantha the others curiosity got the best of them and they were smelling around and snorting at her as well the sorrel horse was the first to start pushing her pack around with his nose as if trying to get into it. Slowly Samantha began to move her hand toward her pack luckily, she had not zipped it shut after she put the plastic bag in it. Slowly she moved her hand toward the opening the sorrel horse blowing off a soft snort as she did so. As she got her hand into the bag and got a firm grip on the piece of salt, she slowly withdrew her hand with the piece of salt in it. The sorrel horse's body squatted and moved back but his feet never moved as she drew the salt out exposing it to the horses, working his nose he wiggled it and slowly licked at the salt trying to bite it away from her hand she held tight amazed at how strong the end of his nose could be. After the first lick the sorrel horse gave up all caution and the streak faced bay began pushing his way in for some of the precious commodity. The three mares stood well back not at all sure about what was going on the two roan mares watched nervously from a safe distance not sure what to think of this new creature. Soon she felt comfortable enough to slowly reach out and touch the sorrel horse on the nose he took it all in stride and continued to lick and bite at the piece of salt. It was almost a competition with the two the sorrel and the streak face bay horse and pretty soon she was rubbing them around their ears and as they tried to gobble up the salt. Since the first time that she had seen the horses several weeks ago now they had gained a lot weight their ribs and hips were not sticking out as far they had not completely shed all of their ling winter hair they still looked a little rough but they were on the mend and fresh green grass was starting to do it's part.

The two roan mares had lost interest and had moved off to a safe distance the three older mares would liked to of had a go at the salt but just didn't have enough trust in the human. The two geldings were all in they had no problem getting friendly with the human for some of her salt. The horses hung around the tree trunk and the girl for a long time the two geldings seemed to be enjoying the attention of the human. The setup could not have been more perfect the horses had discovered Samantha in a non threatening way by not being alarmed they had moved their way into her space letting their curiosity instead of their flight mode take over, it had worked our well and Samantha played her hand to perfection. Had they blundered into each other and surprised the other it might have taken several days or weeks for them to be curious enough to come back and lick the salt from her hand. When Samantha took ready to leave the two geldings followed her for a short distance. The three older mares kept a safe distance but didn't move, the two roan mares raised their heads high and moved off ready to flee at any sudden move or sound. Samantha was very careful not to make any sudden movements taking each step slow and steady. She continued to move off slowly until she had worked her way up the slope out of the creek bottom onto the open country once she was out of site of the horses she broke into a run she was so excited that she could not possibly walk to her house. She would run as far as she could then she would walk for a while letting herself catch her breath, then she was running again. Her mother had seen her running toward the house and she felt fear thinking that there was something wrong and that was why she was running. Her mother met her at the lower gate the girl out of breath and excited tried to tell her mother what had happened to her with the horses. It took several minutes to get her calmed down enough that her mother could understand what she was even talking about. That evening at the supper table she repeated the story to her dad as they ate their supper. Even though he was amused and entertained he didn't seem to share the same level of excitement that her and her mother had shared. He said maybe the horses weren't as wild as everyone was saying that they were. Maybe they actually belonged to someone, That is when Samantha told them about the story that the quiet man Keith from up at the head of the valley had told her, then she said that the bay mare and the two brown mares were for sure the ones that had been in the truck when it rolled down the ravine and she was sure that the two roan mares were the results of the old roan stallion long ago, as for the two geldings nobody had ever said anything about losing them. It was a cinch though that they had been somebodies horses and they were gentle and friendly. Finally her dad agreed to not say anything about them that would make anyone want to catch them or chase them away and he would listen for any rumors about the horses.

    The next morning Samantha was up early helped with the breakfast dishes then she was on her way to the creek looking for the band of horses her pocket full of chunks of salt and a sandwich. The horses were not far from where she had left them the afternoon before, their heads down grazing on the fresh green grass near the grove of big cottonwoods. She was careful not to make any sudden moves and startle the horses, instead she stood and waited until they looked at her for a while then went back to grazing, then she would move in a little closer each time. After she had reached a respectable distance from them she sat down on the trunk of a downed cottonwood and there she waited and watched the horses grazing on the green grass. Finally after what seemed longer than it was the sorrel gelding raised his head and made his way over to her, he was not disappointed she had a small chunk of salt in her hand ready for him. He approached her with a great deal more confidence today than he had, had the day before, he went straight to her hand and when she offered him the chunk of salt he took it, crunching loudly as he ate the salt. The other horses hearing the loud crunching raised up their heads and gathered around hoping some would fall to the ground and they could pick it up later. Only the two roan mares didn't come up close instead they stood their ground not moving off as they had done the day before. The streak faced bay gelding made his way to the front of the line and took a chunk of the salt from her hand when she offered it to him, the two brown mares even came in close enough for a good sniff of her sleeve one of them the one with the snip on her nose sniffed and muzzled some of the salt in her hand when she extended it toward her, getting some of the salt on her lip she raised here nose in the air and curled her lip up towards the sky. Then she came back for a better taste this time licking the palm of her hand spilling most of the salt on the ground. The horses pushed around until they had eaten all of her salt or it was spilled on the ground. After a long while the horses began grazing again moving off toward the creek where they all went and got a long drink of the cold water.

Almost everyday for spring break it was the same for Samantha, she would help her mother clean up the breakfast dishes then she was on her way to the creek bottom hoping to find the band of horses. Most days she was able to find the horses and they would let her be near them as they grazed the two gelding actually letting her scratch them on their withers and on their heads around their ears they liked that a lot. The rest accepted her but kept their distance from her, the horses shedding of the long thick winter coat in exchange for the sleek and shiny summer coat. The spring break was over all to soon and the girl was riding the bus to the school where she would set in the classroom thinking about the band of horses that were on the creek bottom near the grove of big cottonwoods. Hopefully she could make it down to the creek once or twice a week for the next few weeks and hopefully the horses would stay around until summer.

Samantha true to her promise to herself did manage to make it down to the creek at least once a week during the week most weeks and she was always there at least one day on the weekends, the horses grew accustom to her being around they would hardly even look up when she walked toward them anymore. She was like the little black birds that flew and fluttered around the horses feet as their were grazing, they were not bothered by her at all.

Samantha made it through the rest of the school year, counting the days until summer vacation started. When that day finally rolled around she was more than happy to bid her classmates farewell and climb on the bus, she already had plans made in her head she just needed to get home. As the bus pulled away from her yard she watched thoughtfully thinking about everything she wanted to do for the summer. Her and her mom had been doing a lot of talking about getting themselves a couple of nice horses that they could ride together. Her dad was even beginning to see what a good idea it was kinda in his own way.

CHAPTER
Sixteen

To her dismay the first day of summer was a cold heavy overcast rainy day and so were the next four days. Samantha and her mom had cleaned just about every square inch of the house and they were talking about taking on the barn when the sun finally came out. Then with two more days of drying out enough so that they were able to walk around without sinking up to their ankles. Because of end of year obligations at school and now with five days of rain then two more to dry out it had been over two weeks since Samantha had made it down to the grove of big cottonwoods down by the creek. She was anxious to go see the horses, she was also hoping that they were still there.

Samantha was up early ready to be on her way down to the creek it was hard for her to help with the morning mess she was wanting to leave so bad. Finally everything was done and she was off heading down the old cow trail going straight to the grove of big cottonwoods. After all of the rain the grass was heavy with dew the drops covering the tall grass causing it lay over from the weight of the moisture. By the time she reached the grove of cottonwoods her shoes were soaked through and she could feel her socks becoming wet from the dew. The sun was getting warmer as it made it's way up into the sky, she knew that would just be a matter of time before before everything was dried completely out. When she reached the creek the horses were no where to be found, she went down the creek for a good ways and then she went up the creek looking for the horses still not having any luck. She had been able to find tracks and sign that to her looked like it fresh maybe from yesterday. Finally after she was about to give up and go back home she caught a glimpse of a tail of one of the horses swishing at a fly, way up in a side canyon one she had never been up before. It was getting late and she was tired from all of the walking that she had already done so she decided to make her way back to her house and try again tomorrow. The walk back was a pleasant one the ground and the grass drying out and smelling fresh after the rain, the sun was warm as it started across the western sky. She walked back thinking about the horses wondering how much longer they could go before either they went back to where they had come from or somebody decided that they needed to be put into captivity or disposed of in any number of ways. Ways that she didn't like t think about. She got home did her chores and then went up to her room, she had a lot of things to think about.

After the supper dishes had been cleaned up Samantha went back up to her room, there was an idea coming to life in her head and she wanted to think about it some more before she presented it to her mom and dad. Maybe if she slept on it it would manifest into an idea that was good for everyone.

Samantha had been very drawn to and intrigued by the horses both by their beauty and their behavior. It got to the point that if the horses were anywhere near the creek bottom or the grove of big cottonwoods you could find Samantha near by. She became a very good student of the horses she began to notice different types of behavior and unique characteristics of each individual horse. She would look at and study the ground looking at their tracks and soon she was able to recognize some of the hoof prints of some of the horses. She began to have names for them and she always tried to get as close as she possibly could and yet not frighten the horses away. As she learned more about the ways that the horses reacted to things around them she began to simulate what she had seen and she was able to get closer and stay there longer without them becoming alarmed or uneasy about her being there. As time went on the horses became more and more comfortable with the presents of the girl and she was able to sometimes even walk among them but not touching them. When the horses moved Samantha would follow walking as close as she could as they traveled and grazed during the day.

Since Samantha had chores to do she would have to leave before dark in time that she could have her chores all done before supper time. Even though she had other things to do the horse were never very far from her mind, they were about the only thing that she could think about. The nights were full of dreams of wild horses and being among them. When the morning would come she would hurry up and finish her chores and then she was back looking for the horses and being with them.

After a night of restless sleep Samantha made her way downstairs not quite as early as the previous days, breakfast was ready and her dad had already eaten and left for his day at work, that just left her and her mom. That would be better her mom would maybe have an opinion about the idea that had been brewing in her head for the last couple of days. She was quiet as she ate her breakfast and her mom left her to her silence. After she finished her breakfast she cleaned off the table and washed the dishes then she told her mom that she had an idea and she wanted her to hear it. Her mom ask her what was on her mind and that is when she began telling her about the idea that she had come up with. She began with the idea that they had been talking about getting a couple of horses, to which her mother agreed then she went on to tell her more about the two gelding that were running with the wild mares. She told her how gentle and friendly they were and that she was sure that she could catch them easily enough if she were to take a couple of halters with her sometime.

Her mother listened until she had finished then she said "you seem to have this all figured out", but there are other things to consider first off the two gelding had belonged to somebody before they became part of the little band of horses. She went on to say with a smile "you know they used to hang people that took other peoples horses". She commented that was a good idea, but they knew nothing about the background of either of the horses just because they were friendly and gentle didn't mean that they were safe to be ridden". She agreed that she would help her look into any outstanding claims mentioning any lost horses that fit the description of the two geldings. She also said that maybe they should try to get them caught and brought up to the barn so that they would be available in the event that someone did claim them and wanted them back. That would also keep the attention off of the older mares and the two roan mares. Her mom agreed that they should start making a plan to get the two gelding caught and brought up to the pens at the barn. She said that she needed to go to town tomorrow and that she would pick up some bags of sweet feed from the feed store while she was there.

That night after supper was finished and the mess was all cleaned up they sprung the idea on her dad which to their surprise he was in favor of the whole thing, stating that if someone was looking for the two geldings they would probably like to have them back. So it was decided that tomorrow her mom would pick up the grain while she was in town, and the next few days would be spent working on bringing in the two gelding, her mom agreed to help. It was Samantha's job to clean out the old water trough and have it full of fresh clean water, that way it would be there if they got the geldings to the corral. That night it was difficult for her to go to sleep she was excited with the idea of bringing in the two gelding, having two horses in the pens at the barn was a dream come true. Finally she slept and the horses ran through her dreams wild and free.

The next morning Samantha woke up early and she went down stairs her dad was already gone and her mom was busy getting things ready for her trip to town. They cleaned up and washed the dishes from their breakfast then her mom thought it would be a good idea to go to the tack room and see what kind of halters were there. She was sure that there would be plenty and that they would be good, her uncle had always had good tack, but she just wanted to check and make sure. After her inspection she picked out two fairly new looking rope halters with nice long lead ropes, she shook the dust off of them and hung them from a peg near the door, then she walked over to the grain bin raised the lid and looked inside. It was empty and clean she was glad to see she had been dreading looking thinking that it may be full of mice and their residue. Next she looked around until she found two plastic feed buckets with good handles, these she set these next to the grain bin. After she was satisfied with what she found at the barn and tack room she went back to the house washed her hands and then she was off for her errands in town leaving Samantha to her job of cleaning the water trough.

When her mom returned from town that afternoon Samantha had the water trough clean and it was filling with fresh water, her mom drove her truck down to the barn and together they unloaded the grain and put it into the grain bin. It was then that her mom told her that she thought it would be a good idea for her to go with her until they had caught the two geldings. Samantha was happy with the idea that her mom would be going with her when she went looking for the horses in the morning, they would have a good day together. For the rest of the afternoon they worked around the barn and the compound cleaning up and doing little chores that they had been meaning to do. They were not sure how long this was going to take to bring the two geldings here to the pens, away from the mares that they had been with for so long.

The next morning there was a twinge of excitement in the air as they ate their breakfast, everything was the same except that her mother had on a long sleeve shirt and a pair of well worn hiking boots. With breakfast out of the way they put some sandwiches and some water into Samantha's backpack and then they went to the barn put some grain in the two plastic bucket and grabbed the two halter from the peg near the door and they were on their way. Her mom was pretty sure that it would take more than one day to accomplish this chore, but she also knew that if everything lined up they needed to be prepared. The sun was warm and they talked about the different plants and the fact that they might not even see the band of horses today. As they approached the rim of the canyon that went down into the creek above the grove of big cottonwoods they became quiet, looking out across the open country on the other side and looking down into the creek bottom itself they did not want to startled the horse by coming upon them to sudden like. Her mom also was aware of the fact that with her there it was going to be very different for the horses especially the ones that were not as trusting toward humans as the two geldings were. Today their plan was to find the horses get the two geldings to eating the grain and get her mom introduced to the horses, and let them start getting used to her being around. They were sure that the presents of another human would send up all kinds of red flags making the horses suspicious of everything that was happening.

It had been a long time since her mother had been down to the creek and to the grove of big cottonwoods, she had forgotten how pretty and peaceful the place was. This had always been one of her favorite places to go when she was with her uncle. She was glad that her daughter had found this place and that it was a special place for her as well. They stood at the rim the sun warm on their shoulders, looking up and down the creek for any signs of the band of horses before they made their way down into the bottom. After they were certain that the horses were not anywhere near and that they weren't going to surprise them they slowly made their way down into the creek bottom. The trail was steep and rocky so they took their time not wanting to slip and maybe spill any of the grain from the buckets that they carried.

Once they reached the creek bottom the going was much easier, first they walked over to the grove of big cottonwoods where they spent a few minutes looking for any fresh sign that might have been there. When they were satisfied that the horses had not been there anytime recently they moved on always looking for any sign that might be fresh. When Samantha told her mom about the side canyon that she had last seen the horses in they decided that they should go straight to there and begin their search. It was a little bit of a hike to get to the mouth of the side canyon, but as soon as they started up it they began seeing tracks that looked somewhat fresh. A little further up the sign grew fresher and they began to feel some excitement about the project that they had begun. As they moved up the canyon it began to open up with grass covered bottoms. As they worked their way up the little canyon they started to see pools of clear water this was why the horses had not been coming out everything that they needed was up this little side canyon. They were seeing a lot more fresh sign so they cautiously made their way around a bend as they did so they came into view of nice little grove of cottonwoods. There standing in the shade and grazing on the grass that was under the trees they spotted the band of horses.

Here they stopped and watched for a few minutes talking in low voices about how they thought what the best approach would be from here. It was agreed that the girl should go forward and see if she could get the geldings to eating grain from her bucket, her mother would stay out of sight in a place that she could see what was going on and if it looked okay she would make her way over to the tree with her bucket of grain and see what happened next.

Samantha moved off in plan sight of the horses walking slowly and talking as she went. The blue roan mare was the first to notice her, she raised her head ears pointed straight at the girl, her nostrils flared standing still as a statue. One by one the other horses raise their heads until all of them were looking at the girl focusing all of their attention on this human that was slowly walking toward them. Samantha stopped and continued to talk to the horses, the bay roan mare acted the most nervous moving around to the back of the other horses, putting all of them between her and the girl. As the horses became more relaxed the girl slowly worked her way in closer careful not to make any sudden moves that might startle the horses and make them want to leave. Samantha moved in until she thought that she could see the bay mare looking like she was getting ready to move away. There she stood with the bucket of grain her hand slowly she raised the bucket and with her other hand she scooped up some of the grain pouring it back into the bucket, hoping that it would put the scent of the sweet smelling grain into the air.

The sorrel gelding was the first to step toward her his nostrils working trying to get a better smell of the grain. Slowly his feet began to move taking him toward the girl, the bay gelding made his way from out of the middle of the group to the edge where he stopped and raised his head his nose sniffing the air looking at the girl as she continued to scoop the grain. The sorrel gelding moved up closer to Samantha the scent of the grain getting stronger as he did so. He stopped just out of reach of Samantha stretching his nose out as far as her could trying to get close enough to take a bite of the grain from the bucket. Samantha offer him the bucket and he blew softly as he placed his nose in the bucket nibbling with his lip and finally taking a small bite then raising his head and pulled away. He nodded his head as he mouthed the small bit of grain that he had grabbed dropping most of it on the ground, then he raised his nose up into the air and curled up his upper lip.

The bay gelding came closer moving past the sorrel gelding, bolder and less cautious he walked up to the girl and stuck his nose into the bucket and took a mouth full of the grain and began chewing it right in the bucket, then greedily shoving his nose down into the bucket so hard that Samantha almost dropped the bucket and took another bite even before he was finished with the first one. With the boldness of the bay gelding to reassure him the sorrel gelding moved back in closer putting his nose into the bucket and taking a bite of the sweet grain and began chewing it as the bay gelding pushed him away going in for another mouth full. Samantha was ready for him and she braced herself as he shoved his nose into the bucket.

When the bay gelding had started eating grain out of the bucket, her mom had started slowly making her way toward the horses and her daughter, fully aware that the horses could knock the girl down and step on her trying to get the grain. Her plan was working fine and she was closing the distance, as she moved she watched the other horses that weren't eating grain, but they seemed to be focused on the two geldings and the girl and they paid her no mind. When she was just a few feet behind the girl she spoke letting her know that she was close and for her to back away toward her and they could stand together and let the horses eat from both buckets. As the girl moved next to her mom, her mom noticed that her bucket was almost empty the two geldings had gone after the grain in a big way. As soon as they were next to each other the bay gelding reached into her mom's bucket and took a big bite of her grain, he acted as if he was starving the way he went after the grain.

While her mom held her bucket of grain with one hand she tried to pet or scratch the head of the geldings with her other hand hoping to get them used to the idea and then she could get a lead rope around one of their necks and then be able to get a halter on. The horses proved to be to skeptical and suspicious of the new human so they just let them eat all of the grain from their buckets, it was a good start. After all of the grain was gone the geldings were a little cranky laying their ears back at each other and pawing at the buckets where they had set them down, but they would not let either the girl or her mother walk up to them. They stayed with the horses for a good length of time letting them become familiar with the second human, the only ones that really acted like they even cared were the two roan mares, they stayed to the back careful to keep the older mares between them and the humans. They slowly walked around and stood as close to the mares as they dared and not making them move away. Her mom was impressed with the quality of the mares they were a really nice well put together group of horses. To good of quality to be roaming around unclaimed, as for the two gelding they were two well made horses as well someone had, had a good eye when they got them.

After an hour or so the girls decided that they should be heading back home and start preparations for tomorrow. They picked up the buckets that the two geldings had scattered around and they began walking down the canyon, the two gelding following them as they did so. They followed them almost down to the spot where her mother had waited for her while she walked up to the horses. There the gelding stopped and watched as they continued to walk away then together they spun around bucking and racing back to the little band of mares. Once they reached the mares they all fell in with them and ran a little ways up the canyon before they stopped and began grazing on the green grass. The way they looked had completely changed since the first time the girl had seen them. Then they were then and weak, shaggy with their long winter coats still in place, now they were fat and slick and full of energy. The green grass had done it's job.

They talked as they walked back home they were both excited about how the day had gone for them. It didn't seem to take any time at all before they walked into their yard. The sun was getting low in the sky to the west as they arrived, they quickly did their chores then went inside there they washed up and began making supper, it had been a long day and they were both tired and hungry. When her dad got home they told him about their day. After her mom told him about the horses and how impressed she had been with the quality of them all, he seemed to start warming up to the idea of bringing the two geldings in and he shared their excitement. Wishing them the best of luck for the following day on their quest to bring in the two geldings.

The next morning they were all up early having breakfast and then cleaning up before they all left. Her dad was working on a big irrigation project for a local farmer way down in the lower part of the valley. He would be gone most of the day, but wished them the very best of luck again as he drove out of the yard. They went to the barn retrieved their two halters and put fresh grain into their feed buckets, then they were on their way in search of the band of horses once more. The sun was warm and they walked mostly in silence until they reached the rim above the creek bottom. There they stood looking up and down the creek for any signs of the band of horses, satisfied that they were not anywhere near they made their way down the trail to the bottom from there they went directly to the side canyon where they had left the horses the day before.

Today the horses were not at the grove of little cottonwoods so they made their way further up the little canyon, as they went around a narrow bend to their surprise the canyon opened into a wide meadow with rock rims on both sides. In the creek bed there was pools of water with a small stream flowing between the pools keeping them fresh and cool. It was here that they spotted the horses they were grazing near the canyon wall where the grass was tall and green. As they stood there in awe taking in all of the scenery and the horses her mom was glad that they had made the decision to move to this place and that they no longer lived in the city.

Slowly they started making their way toward the horses stopping every so often watching the horses for any signs of surprise, finally the bay mare raised her head and looked right at them. She stood there head high her nostrils working sniffing the air for any signs of danger. The two geldings raised they heads and actually took a few steps in their direction before stopping and sniffing the air, hoping that there was the smell of sweet grain. The girl and her mom slowly moved closer talking to the horses and careful not to make any sudden moves that would startle the horses. The bay roan mare snorted softly as she moved around behind the horses always keeping them between her and the humans. The blue roan stood her ground but never took her eyes off of the two humans, as for the three older mares they didn't show that much interest, as long as the humans didn't move in to close they were ok about it. They were fully aware that they run away from the humans with very little effort.

Samantha and her mom kept moving closer stopping and letting the two geldings and the mares have time to get comfortable with their presents. Finally the bay gelding began walking toward them the sorrel waited then moved of after him a few yards behind. The bay gelding walked straight up to the girl and shoved his nose down into the bucket taking a big mouthful of the sweet grain. The sorrel gelding coming up and sniffing the bucket waiting for the bay gelding to move away, finally he put his nose into the bucket that her mom was holding and took a small bite of the sweet grain. He stepped away chewing the grain before getting another bite, this time he lingered over the bucket chewing the grain as if he was savoring it. Samantha was able to scratch the bay gelding around his ears as he was eating out of the bucket that she held for him. Slowly her mom was able to rub the sorrel gelding's face and worked her way up to and around his ears, he was a little skeptical at first but soon allowed her to rub and scratch him all over his head and along his neck. She noticed that both of the geldings had welts from bug bites all over their necks and bodies.

The geldings finished eating the grain from their buckets and they let them scratch and rub them on their heads and neck, but every time her mom would try to get around on the side where she could put a halter on they would move off. When they did she would start the process all over again looking for a good place to stop so that they would be in a better place the following day or the next time they approached them. The geldings hung around for a long time seeming to like the company of the two humans. Finally they picked up their buckets and started making their way back down the little canyon, the two geldings following along like two big dogs. The followed longer and further than the day before staying with them almost all the way back to the grove of little cotton woods where they had found them the day before. When the two geldings stopped instead of spinning around and racing and bucking back to the mares they just stood there and watched the two humans walk away until they were out of sight then they dropped their heads and started grazing on the green grass.

Her mom was pleased with how the geldings acted when they left she said it was easy to see that they were thinking more about them and the buckets of sweet grain than they were of the other mares. She was pretty sure that with a few more days maybe even less they could have their halters on the two geldings. As they went across the main creek bottom when they neared the water her mom felt the sharp hot bite of a deer-fly on her arm as she instantly swatted the triangle shaped speckled insect. That was why the horses all had so many welts on them and that was probably why they had moved up into the little side canyon to get away from these blood sucking flies. When they got to the top of the rim above the creek bottom it seemed that all of the biting insects had stayed back near the water.

The walk home was a pleasant one the girl and her mom talking about the horses and wondering where they might have came from and if their previous owners were even still looking for them. It was a warm afternoon and they were feeling the strength of the sun as they walked along the old cow trail. When they came into the yard her dad was already home his truck was backed into the big doors on the end of the barn. He was just finishing up unloading the load of hay that he had brought home with him. As they walked into the barn the smell of the fresh hay seemed to fill the barn with new life and possibilities. Samantha was now sure that there would soon be two geldings here eating this fresh hay.

Her dad began telling them that while he was down in the valley working on the irrigation project they had baled a field of hay the night before. Knowing that there would probably soon be some horses around they were going to be needing some hay so he made an arrangement to buy some of the hay. Tomorrow he would take the flat bed trailer and bring I back so they could unload it this weekend. They swept the loose hay out of the back of the pickup then they all went to the house, there they took a break with some cool drinks and a snack telling each other about how their day had gone. Later they would go back out and do their evening chores then come back for supper and off to bed later.

The next morning after breakfast they went to the barn the sweet smell of the fresh hay filled the barn, a smell that they enjoyed as they put grain in their buckets and took their halters from the peg by the door and headed to the creek once more, one day closer to bringing the two gelding back to the barn with them. Maybe today was the day. As they walked they talked about different things today her mom was telling her about her uncle and how he had shown her to be patient and had told her many things that had helped her later to understand how horses behaved. If they were able to get the horses today or next week it would take as long as it took all they could do was to set it up and let it happen, when things were ready it would happen. She told to always be looking for the slightest of movements or efforts, these in turn would usually be some of the biggest things that happened. Sometimes they were so subtle that it was easy to miss them. To always be aware of these little things was the beginning of the foundation to working with horses.

When they reached the rim looking down into the creek bottom they stopped and looked up and down the creek bottom for a few minutes before they went down into the bottom. The walked across the bottom jumping across the creek, the sun was warm and the deer flies were hungry along the waters edge. Biting them with sharp hot bites making them slap themselves to either hit the insect or drive them away. As they got further from the water the flies were less intense. They went up the side canyon walking with confidence that they would find the horses near where they had left them the day before. As they approached the small grove of little cotton woods they spotted the horses they were in the shade under the trees standing head to tail swatting the flies from each other.

The bay gelding was the first to spot them he raised his head and began coming their way almost instantly. The sorrel gelding looking the other way soon realized that his buddy had moved out of the shade looked around and followed not far behind. The bay gelding walked up her mother and put his nose into her bucket and took his usual big greedy bite his ears laid back clearly not wanting to share with anybody. The sorrel gelding walked up to Samantha and almost politely put his nose in her bucket and took a bite of the grain. They were able to rub and scratch the gelding all over their heads and along their necks as they ate the grain. They had set the buckets down on the ground and the geldings didn't seem to mind acting like they even liked the all of the attention. As they rubbed and scratched they were talking and her mom was pretty sure that they could get their halters on the gelding, but just to be on the safe side they decided to wait until tomorrow before making an attempt. They wanted to see how the geldings acted when they departed today. The three older mares and the two roan mares only looked at them today none of them wanting to leave the shade of the trees.

The two geldings ate the sweet grain and stood there while they rubbed and scratched around their ears and up under their manes. When they moved down under their the throats into their chest there were lots of bug bites that must have really itched because when the began scratching under there both gelding stretched their heads and necks out as far as they bobbing their heads as they scratched. Her mom was sure that they had hit sweet spot and that they would be friends for life. The expression on the gelding was that of total submission when they decided that they should leave, confident that tomorrow would be the day that they could leave with the two geldings.

The two geldings followed them staying close not wanting them to leave or stop scratching, they followed them almost to the mouth of the little side canyon, once again stopping and watching them as they walked away. When they jumped back across the creek the stopped and looked back the two gelding were both still standing looking at them wanting them to come back and scratch some more. Her mom let out a little laugh saying that those two geldings acted like they missed having humans around.

The walk back home seemed to fly by Samantha was so excited, they talked the whole way both of them pleased with how they had left the two geldings. They were in that place where they wanted more more attention and they were ready to have it. Her mother was certain that if they didn't get them tomorrow for sure the next day. She wanted to be careful not to set the expectations to high so that they had a little room for error after all the odds were in favor of the horses if they decided that they didn't want to get caught.

When they walked into the yard the big barn doors were open and her dad's pickup with the flatbed trailer was backed into the barn. Her dad and another man were just about finished unloading and putting the hay into a neat stack at the end of the barn. The man worked with her dad sometimes when they needed extra help, he was sort of the community handy man. The fragrant smell of the fresh hay was everywhere in the barn. Samantha brought the broom and swept the loose chafe from the bed of the flatbed as the two men finished with the last bale of hay. She was very excited with all of the things that had happened the last few days she was sure that there would be horses here very soon.

That night at the supper table there was lots of discussion about the horses and the irrigation project that her dad was working on. Her mom had put a pot roast with potatoes into a crock-pot before they left this morning and everything was cooked to perfection. Like the barn was full of the fresh smell of hay, the house was full of the smell of the roast making her stomach grumble just from the smell, in all of her excitement she not even though about how hungry she was. After the table had been cleared and the dishes were done Samantha went up to her room and took a shower and then she lay down on her bed. When she woke up her light was still on but the rest of the house was dark and quiet, she got up turned off her light and crawled into bed asleep as soon as her head touched the pillow.

Morning came way to early or so it seemed the gray light of the early morning had already filled her room, she could hear her mom and dad down stairs her mom was making breakfast. She got out of bed got dressed washed the sleep from her eyes and went downstairs. The smell of bacon and pancakes was kind of picked her up and carried her to her place at the table. After they ate the crisp smoky bacon and the light fluffy pancakes they cleared the table and washed the dishes. Her mom sat down and made a list that she gave to her dad so that he could pick up some things from the store before he came home after work. After that they went to the barn, the smell of fresh hay was almost intoxicating they put grain in their buckets and took their halters from the peg by the door and they were on their way to the little side canyon where they had left the horses the day before.

The walk down to the creek seemed longer today Samantha was full of excitement and could hardly wait to get there, finally they reached the rim at the edge of the creek bottom. Once again they stood there for a few minutes looking up and down the creek and into the grove of big cotton woods before going down into the bottom. Today they got a surprise near the edge of the grove of big cottonwoods was a herd of mule deer, several does with their fawns were all grazing on the fresh green grass. Not wanting to disturb them, they watched them for a few minutes before the deer moved off making their way further down the creek bottom. That had been a real treat it was the first time that the girl had seen any deer along the creek.

Once again they went to the place that they always crossed and hopped across the creek and went to the little side canyon and went up to the little grove of little cottonwoods the horses were not there so they continued on up through the narrow bend. As they came out into the big meadow they saw the horses heads down grazing along the shaded side under the rock wall. They stood there watching the horses for a few minutes not wanting to startle them, finally the brown mare with the snip on her nose raised her head and looked at them, the rest of them soon were all looking at them in their usual way. The two geldings edging out of the bunch in their direction they were ready for their sweet grain and the scratching that came with it. As they watched the geldings coming to them her mom took out her halter and made sure it was ready to be put on, as she did Samantha did like wish almost to excited to get the halter untied. They walked toward the geldings as they came toward them meeting somewhere near the middle. The geldings came right up to them full of confidence the bay came to Samantha taking his big greedy first bite of grain from her bucket and the sorrel politely taking his bite from her moms bucket. After they had taken a few bite of the grain and were chewing with their noses in the buckets they set the buckets down on the ground in the grass and began rubbing and scratching the geldings along their necks and withers, careful not to over do it and push them away.

After the geldings had mostly finished the grain they stood there letting them rub and scratch their heads and around their ears. That was when her mom reached her arm across the sorrel geldings neck and reached under his throat grabbed the end of the halter and held the nose piece out offering it to him, waiting, careful not to over whelm him all at once. The gelding stood there for a few seconds and then he stuck his nose into the halter, her mom tied the end over his head. Samantha had followed her mom lead she had her arm over the bay gelding neck and was waiting for him to place his nose into the halter when her mom told her to go a head and put the halter. The bay horse was ready to be caught but he wasn't going help out the process. Samantha tied the halter and looked at her mom her eyes asking now what? Her mom answered her by saying now all they had to do was lead them home. With one last look at the little band of mares her mom took off down the canyon the sorrel gelding following willingly the girl falling in behind the bay gelding stood for a second as she tugged on the lead then he to followed along. As she looked back the little band of mares stood watching them as the led the gelding through the narrow bend and down the little canyon.

They went past the little grove of little cottonwood trees, the two geldings following along with no problems at at all. They did really well until they came to the mouth of the little canyon, there the sorrel gelding stopped and looked back up the little canyon. Her mother stopped and waited keeping a slight tension on the lead rope after a few seconds the sorrel gelding moved out again keeping step with her mom. The bay gelding seemed to happy just to be going along, the next place that they were to sure about was going to be the creek crossing it self. When they reached the creek crossing her mother instead of jumping like they had been doing she just took an extra long step getting both feet a little wet in the process, but the sorrel gelding never wavered he just stepped across like he did it everyday that way. The bay gelding followed Samantha even though she hopped across the creek, he followed her like a big puppy. As they came to the creek the deer flies got thicker and more aggressive landing on the geldings ears, necks and all over their faces. Samantha and her mom stopping to brush the flies away then on their way again the geldings trying to rub on their faces on their shoulders to keep the flies away. They led the horses up the trail to the top of the rim at the top of the rim they stopped and brushed away any flies that were still on the geldings. After a couple of minutes they started toward the barn, the geldings willing to follow as if they were ready to be back in the human world. The whole trip back home was uneventful they just walked like they usually did and the gelding kept step with them. As they got closer to the yard the gelding's heads came up and their ears pointed forward and it seemed that their pace quickened a bit, the bay gelding nickered in the direction of the barn hoping for an answer. They were eager to be coming into the barn area, they led them straight to the pen with the lean to next to the barn with the big hay rack underneath the lean to. Her dad had put some fresh hay in the big rack before he had left for work this morning, the water trough was clean and full of fresh water, they led them into the pen stopped and scratched their sweaty ears and the they took the halters off and walked out of the pen. The geldings dropping their heads and softly snorting and sniffing along the ground it was the first time they had been in the security of a corral in several years.

Samantha and her mother stood on the outside of the gate looking back through the pipes at their accomplishment. It had taken them four days, but their patience had paid off they had caught the two geldings and brought them to the barn without incident. The excitement the girl had been feeling for so long had changed to the satisfaction of a job well done, and she was tired. Now that they had got the gelding into the confinement of the corral they would have to start the pain staking process of trying to find the true owners of the geldings. That was a job for another day, right now they just wanted to finish up their outside chores and go celebrate their accomplishment with a cool drink and a soft chair.

When her dad came home they all went down to the barn to look at the geldings. They were standing under the lean to munching on the fresh hay they seemed content to be in the pen and under a roof. He agreed that the geldings showed good breeding, but there were no brands on either of them so it might be difficult to find out who they really belonged to. He said he had made a couple of phone calls and what he had been told was that they needed to get in touch with the local sate brand inspector and he could advise them on what steps they should take, he said he would call him tomorrow. After looking at the geldings for a while they made sure that they had plenty of fresh hay for the night. Then they went back to the house and had a meal of their own.

CHAPTER
Seventeen

The next morning her dad called the local brand inspector and explained the situation to him, he told her dad that he would be out to look at the two geldings and do the proper paper work the following afternoon. After agreeing on a time her dad hung up the phone and told them that they would be able to maybe find out more about the two geldings. At any rate in would be interesting to hear what the inspector had to say. For the next day and a half Samantha could hardly stay away from the barn and the two gelding that now occupied the pen and the lean to with the big hay rack. The geldings seem to enjoy the attention that they were getting from her, they would stand and let her brush them not minding at all.

The brand inspector arrived at the time that he had agreed to, her mom going out to greet him and introduce herself his name was Larry. They visited as they walked over to the barn Samantha following along hoping to herself that they didn't have to take the two geldings away. They walked into the pen the inspector walking around the horses looking at them from all sides, looking for some form of identification a brand or a scar or something that would define them. To his dismay there was nothing, he then went into a story that happened a couple of years ago when the big fire burned the other side of the mountain.

There had been two out of state hunters that had come up from Texas on a scouting trip because they had drawn once in a life time tags to hunt in a normally restricted area. They thought it would be a good idea to come up a few weeks prior and get familiar with the country. They had driven as far as they could back into one of the remote camp grounds as close as they could get to the area that they were suppose to hunt in later in the fall. They had ridden and hiked for a few days they had used most of there groceries, they weren't ready to leave yet so they had decided to stay a few more days, so they tied up one of the geldings leaving the other graze around at liberty. They had taken their pickup and trailer and went into to which was about three hours away. While they were gone was when the storm that started the fire blew in. The storm was a hot one with lots of wind and the lightening was striking all over the mountain one of the fires starting only a few hundred yards from where the horse was tied. Nobody really knows if the fire or the lightning caused the horse that was tied to panic and pull back until he finally broke the lead rope, joining the already loose horse and together they ran. They ran away from the storm and the blazing fire. The fire did come right through where the horses had been, but when the two men returned everything around the camp site had burned there was a piece of rope hanging from the tree that the one gelding had been tied to. The men stayed around for a few days looking and hoping that they would find the two geldings, but the fire had driven them miles away into some other part of the mountain. They had finally determined that the fire may have overtaken the geldings in some rugged terrain and they had been consumed by the fire. Because of the fire burning almost the entire area where they had planned to hunt they never returned. That had been almost three years ago, it would be hard to say if these were even the same horses. The campsite that they were at is over one hundred and fifty miles as a crow flies from right here. That is a long ways and there is a lot of wild country between here and there.

The brand inspector took out two pieces of paper each one having the outline of a horse looking both ways as well as front and a back view. Slowly he walked around each horse again this time drawing in all of the marking of each horse on the outline on the papers. After that was done wrote a brief description of each horse and where the horse had been found. He then said that he would have to advertise the two geldings for thirty days, anyone claiming them would have to have proof of ownership, a bill of sale, a photograph, or a registration paper, even a notarized statement had been known to satisfy the head of the livestock board.

Her mom ask the inspector what if nobody claims them? The inspector then said that they are usually auctioned off to the highest bidder hopefully for enough to pay for the cost of the feed that it took to feed them while they were being held with a little extra for administration fees of all the advertising and the paperwork. Then she ask where they usually held them at he told her that they had an arrangement with a fellow down at the end of the valley, but there was nothing saying that they couldn't stay right here if they wanted to take on the responsibility, saying they would be reimbursed for their feed and troubles. Her mom told him that they would like to do that if that was a possibility, she also told him that they would be interested in making the purchase if and when the time came. He agreed saying that would save him bringing a trailer back and picking them up and hauling them down to the lower valley. It was agreed that the geldings could stay there and the inspector would keep them up to speed about any claims being made. They walked back to the inspectors pickup and talked for a few minutes then he drove off back down the county road toward town. Her mother looked over at Samantha and said "I guess now we wait".

Later that night out of nowhere it seemed a strong thunderstorm blew in waking Samantha from a very sound sleep. There was a lot of thunder and lightning and the rain slammed into the side of the house slapping the windows with sheets of rain, the wind almost shaking the house the gust were so strong. The storm only lasted about a half an hour before moving quickly across the valley.

The next morning there were puddles standing everywhere, the rain had not lasted that long, but it had dumped out a lot of water. After breakfast Samantha went down to check on the two geldings throwing them a little more of the fresh sweet smelling hay. The geldings had thoroughly enjoyed the rain they were both covered on both side with dry mud from rolling out in the middle of the big pen. Their manes were matted with dry mud and there tails had picked up plenty as well, it was going to be a chore to clean them up again. There was still a lot of water standing in the middle of the corral so the girl thought it might be the bast idea to wait until ti had dried up a little bit before cleaning them off again just in case they decide to roll in the mud again. Instead she wanted to go back to the creek bottom and look for the little band of horses that had stayed behind.

She told her mom what her plans were and ask her if she wanted go to. Her mom told her having been away for those few days, she had some things that she needed to get done. Samantha left walking through the wet grass along the trail over the wet ground everything smelling fresh from the rain. When she got to the rim overlooking the creek bottom she stopped and looked up and down the creek, down into the grove of big cottonwoods, and across the other side out into the big flat that was past the creek. Not seeing anything she made her way down into the creek bottom. She went to their crossing at the creek jumped across then went straight to the little side canyon they had last seen the little band of mares. She walked up past the grove of little cottonwoods through the narrow bend and out into the open meadow with the rock rims. She had fully expected to see the mares grazing out in the meadow, but the meadow was empty. She walked on up the canyon not seeing any tracks or sign the rain had erased all of the sign it was difficult to even tell if the horses had even been there. She went on up the canyon as she went the canyon grew rougher and more narrow until she was convinced that no horse could go any further up the little canyon. Confused she turned around and retraced her steps this time looking for someplace where the mares might have made their way out of the canyon. She could not find anything as she came to the mouth of the canyon she looked up and down trying to tell if they came out this way and if so what direction did they go. She walked up the creek bottom looking for some sort of clue but it seems as if they had just vanished the hard rain had washed away all of the tracks. She looked for a couple of hours not finding anything she made her way back across the creek getting swarmed by deer flies she ran to the trail and went up the trail to the top of the rim as fast as she could swatting the stinging flies as she went.

The horses were gone they had left just like they had came unannounced and with no warning and, they had left no clues as to where they were going. Had they went back into mountains where they had came from? Had they went down to the lower end of the valley like they had done before? Samantha spent all morning and finally early in the afternoon discouraged she gave up and went home it was as if the earth had just swallowed them up. She walked back home completely consumed by her thoughts trying to figure out where the little band of horses had gone, it was a mystery and they had not left one clue on how to solve it. Finally she decided that she would give it a few days before returning to the creek bottom and maybe they would have returned or maybe someone would have seen them by then. Either way she had to clean off the adobe armor that the two geldings were covered with, that was going to take a while.

CHAPTER
Eighteen

The little band of mares watched as the two gelding went to the two humans, they watched as the two geldings ate the sweet grain from the buckets that they held. They watched as the two humans got their halters on the two geldings and led them away. They stood watching them as they went through the narrow bend in the canyon and out of site. The bay mare stood watching even after the geldings and he humans were out of site. She put her head down and grazed on the green grass for a few minutes then she raised her head up and followed down the canyon she went through the narrow bend and past the grove of little cottonwoods all the way down to the mouth of the canyon the rest of the little band mares following as she did so. At the mouth of the canyon she stopped and looked in the direction that the two geldings had been taken. She put her head down and took a few bites of the grass that was at her feet. She raised her head chewing the green grass once again looking in the direction that the geldings had been taken. She stood there swishing her tail, shaking her head and stomping her feet at the biting deer flies, as if to be pondering what she was going to do next. She chewed the grass some more then she turned up the creek bottom there was an old cow trail that ran along the creek bottom. She moved onto it and broke into a slow trot the four other mares following close behind. They trotted for several miles before coming to a barbed wire fence that went across the creek bottom. Here she stopped there was a trail that ran along the fence leading out of the creek bottom toward the mountain, she went that way. Walking up the steep slope until they reached the top of the rim then she went into a trot again following the trail that ran along the fence.

They followed the fence moving at a trot until the terrain became to steep to trot then they settled down to a good walk climbing further up the mountain slope. As they climbed the trail grew more rocky and steep soon they were in the timber the trees casting shade on the trail blocking the heat from the sun. The mares bodies covered with sweat the sweat running down their flanks and their front legs their side heaving from the exertion of the climb. The trail sometimes staying close to the fence other times it was well away from the fence but always going up. After well over an hour of climbing up the steep trail they finally came to the top of the ridge here the terrain became mostly an open flat with a good covering of old dry grass. The fence ran across the flat and disappeared into the timber on the other side, the little band of mares moved across the flat and into the timber on the other side. Here the trail grew dim and steep it was really not much of a trail at all, they began climbing again the bay mare continued to follow the fence. They went higher up the side of the mountain the bay mare determined to reach the top, the rest of the little band of mares followed. Somewhere in their climb the fence that they had been following had ended, but the dim trial continued to work it's way up the steep ridge.

As the shadows were getting long the little band of mares made their way to the top of the ridge and out into the big meadow that was at the top. The bay mare led them straight to a small stream that ran through the meadow the mares lined up and drank, they took a long much needed drink. The day had been long and hot and they had traveled far. After they had satisfied their thirst part of them found an area of bare ground and there they laid down and rolled drying the sweet that was still on their bodies. After they shook the loose dirt from their backs they put their heads down and grazed on the tall grass into the cool of the evening. Late that night the wind came of carrying the smell of rain soon the flash of lightning and the rumble of thunder could be seen and heard as a late night thunder storm made it's way across the valley down below. The mares smelled the air and looked in the direction of the thunder and the lightning with only mild interest, they felt safe here on this big meadow. While down below in the valley the storm came with a force and fury at the big meadow on came a nice rain shower. The rain felt good on the mares the sweat that was caked on the hair soften and mixed with rain running down their legs on the ground cleansing their soft summer coat of sweat and dirt. When rain ended the mares shook the water from their hides, their tired muscles feeling better after their long hot day of travel. Somewhere deep down inside her, the bay mare had been growing a primal need to return to her home it was an instinct that was deep inside of her like the one that makes geese fly south in the winter, they don't know why they just do. In the bay mares case she felt the need to be at the place where she had learned her first life's lessons the place where she had felt safe the place where she had been born.

As the sun peaked over the horizon the mares were already grazing on the tall green grass the grass covered with dew from the rain shower in the night before. The mares faces and legs wet from the grass soon the mares had their fill of the good grass and they began walking around looking around this old familiar yet new place. The bay mare and both of the brown mares had all been born in this big meadow, back when the ranch still ran a lot of horses this had been the place were they put the mares to foal, later they would turn out a stallion and here the life would begin again. It had been several years since they had put any horses in the big meadow mostly in more resent years it had been used for a place to summer their yearly steers, but this year it was left empty. The fall before the cattle market had been very good and the demand was so that after much deliberation and crunching numbers it had been decided to sell the steers and safe the grass on the big meadow. Because they had not put any cattle on the big meadow this summer there had been very little to no human presence in the big meadow.

As the mares were exploring the big meadow along the edge of the timber on a rocky out cropping they came across a large wooden box that had part of two white salt blocks still in it. The salt had been left over from the last time that there had been cattle pastured on the big meadow. It had been left for the deer or elk or whatever wild life might come along and want some salt. They had gotten a few bites that had fallen to the ground when the girl had given salt to the geldings, the older mares would always come in after the girl was gone and sniff out the small chunks that the girl might have dropped. After the hot and hard day of travel from the day before their bodies were in need of just such a find, the mares gathered around licking and biting off small pieces of the white block. The two roan mares had never tasted salt before and after they got their first taste they almost went crazy, greedily trying to eat as much as they could, finally their tongues and lips sore and dried out the left the wooden box and went back to the stream and drank their fill of the cool water once again. They soon returned to the wooden box licking on the white blocks once again. The extended absents of salt had given their bodies a craving for the white blocks. They returned to the wooden box with the white salt blocks several times over the next few days consuming much of the two pieces of the two salt blocks, until finally their bodily needs for the mineral being satisfied.

Keith the tall, slender man with the bowed legs had made a long circle horseback when he decided that he would make a swing through the big meadow on his way back down the mountain to the headquarters.

He had left early that morning the stars were still out and the moon had not yet made it's way across the western sky. This time of year he made several trips a week up to the summer country where the cows and calves spent their summer. It was usually and all day kind of a circle this time of year he would usually make it back to the barn close to sundown, turning loose a very tired and hungry horse, he himself tired and hungry as well. About once a month he would take a couple of pack horses with him and he would spent the day packing and restocking salt boxes from what they called the salt shack. It was just an old barn that was left over from the homestead days, it had been fixed up good enough to keep the salt out of the weather. Early in the season he would make slow bumpy trip up the steep rocky trail that made do as a road he would haul a load of salt up and store it in the salt shack and then over the coarse of the summer he would haul it out with pack horses that he led up from the headquarters. He would usually do this about every two weeks or as needed, sometimes he would spend several days packing out the salt using several horse in the process. Sometimes he would use nine or ten horse in a week always turning them loose tired from the long circles. This was good long circles, wet saddle blankets and good feed was what made good horses. Keith had lived here for most of his adult life and he never got tired of making these circles, the wonder of the mountains always left him amused and in awe of nature.

On this day Keith had not taken any pack horses he had went up to high country to bring back some cattle that had drifted to far down the back side of the mountain. This was something that he had to do several times during the month, the country was so steep and rough that they had never built a fence to hold the cattle, instead they had always just rode the country horseback keeping a close watch for any cattle that might want to drift to far in the wrong direction. Keith had picked a small bunch of cattle on the steep slope and had brought them back to the salt lick and close to water, after which he prowled through as many cattle as he could before needing to start the long ride back down the mountain. There were several different trails that led off of the mountain and he usually would take one of these checking on things as he made his way down the mountain.

For some unexplained reason on this day he had decided to circle around through the big meadow, he had not been through that country since last fall when they had gathered the big steers out of there. It would add several more miles onto his day but the day had gone well and he had plenty of daylight left so he headed over the rough and rocky ridge to the big meadow several rough miles away. He followed the rough and rocky trail out of the country where the cows and calves grazed, at the top there was a rock rim that acted as nature boundary between the two areas. At the top there was a narrow gap in the rim only big enough for a saddle horse to go through there between two trees was a wire gate that someone had put there decades before. Keith dismounted opened the gate led his horse through closed the gate and was on his way once more. Between the rim and the big meadow there was a long stretch maybe two miles or a little more where the country was little steep rocky ridges covered with pine trees and oak brush. The dim trail that led to the big meadow was slow going and if hard to follow sometimes there was no trail at all.

It was late afternoon when Keith rode out of the timber into the big open of the big meadow, he was impressed with how much grass there was and how green it all was. There must have been some rains that came through here that had missed everywhere else, he was thinking to himself "of all years not to be running yearlings here". That was when he spotted the tracks, horse tracks, bare footed horse tracks, then he was thinking that he was not short any of his horses and that he had not put any horse here for several years. So this was why had the unexplained urge to come back though her on his way home, now he understood why he had came this way. What horses were these tracks from, he rode over to the head of the stream that that just seemed to come out of nowhere, at the head there was large pool about two feet deep and several feet across, here he let his horse water. While the horse drank his fill of the cool water the man studied the ground around the stream there he saw numerous horse tracks these tracks were fresh, that was strange, there had not been any horses in the Big Meadow for many years this use to be where they would put the remount mares so they could foal. It had been close to fifteen years since they had even any mares up here for that purpose. There were to many tracks for just one or two horses, this was a small bunch that had found their way into the big meadow.

As Keith rode through the big meadow he kept a sharp eye out, looking for the horses that were roaming around, wanting to see them before they saw him. Finally he saw them he was going up a small rise when he spotted them all that had cleared the top of the rise were his head and maybe his shoulders, his horse was still below the line of site for the horses. They were over at the edge of the big meadow lounging around the wooden salt box that was on the rocky out crop inside the trees a little ways. Here he stopped his horse and sat there looking at the horses there were five of them, a bay two brown ones and then he remembered the young girl named Samantha that had peddled her bike all the way up the valley to talk to him about the wild horses. The two roan mares stood out there was no mistaking the horses even at this distance. He watched them for a long while they seemed to all be in good condition, but then he remembered that she said there had been a sorrel and a bay horse with them. He wondered where they might have gone because they didn't appear to be with the mare any longer. From where he sat they had to be over a quarter of a mile away even from here he could see that the two roan mares were some very impressive horseflesh. As he looked at the two roan mares he wondered to himself if they had ever even seen a human, or any other horses for that matter. He thought they are probably wilder than any deer ever thought about being. The three older mares were pretty easy in the eyes as well, for their age and no telling the kind of life they had, had they looked to be fat slick and in good shape. The power of good genetics.

Keith turned his horse back down the rise careful to keep low in the little draw until he was able to get back into the timber, there he skirted around staying hidden from the view of the mares. He was thankful that the air was dead calm not even a breath of air moved as he rode around the meadow. Deep in his thought Keith rode out of the big meadow taking the steep trail that would lead to the barn way down below. He was completely taken back and amused with the fact that the older mares had come back to the place where they had been foaled so many years ago, never under estimate the power and instinct of nature. Keith made his way down the long slope that led into the pens and the big barn this was the country where he kept all of the his horses on his way through he picked up the horses driving them in front of him on his way to the barn. When he reached the barn he penned the horses and caught two for his day's work tomorrow then he turned the rest of the horses back out to go roam around and graze on the long slope. When Keith reached the big barn he unsaddled his horse put his saddle on it's rack and fed his horse some grain and put some fresh hay in the big hay rack under the lean to for the three horses before going to the house were he would feed and water himself.

CHAPTER
Nineteen

The thirty days that they had to wait to see if anyone was going to claim the two geldings seemed to take forever to Samantha. She was anxious to know if they were going to be able to own the two geldings hoping that no one came to claim them. She had done everything she could think of to help make the time go quicker, but it still seemed to go at a snails pace. She had went back down to the creek bottom once a week for three weeks now, hoping to see the little band of mares but every time that she went it was the same thing. The bottom and the little side canyon were empty of any horses. The grass had grown up and was beginning to head out, the rains had kept the ground washed clean of any tracks it was always obvious that there had not been any horses back down in the creek bottom. She would always walk up to the top of the rim leading out of the creek bottom and stand look at the far off mountains and wonder if the little band of mares had went back to where ever it was they had been before they had come to her valley. It made her a little sad to not have the little band of mares moving up and down and all around the creek bottom she missed seeing them and walking in their among them, this side of the valley had become a lonely place to her. She still had the two geldings, but even that could end any day if they happened to be claimed by their previous owners. Her walk back home was one of the longest she had ever had coming back from the creek bottom.

She had fed and brushed both geldings everyday since her and her mom had caught them and brought them to their pens at the big barn. There had been the one night only a couple of days after they had brought the geldings in that the big thunderstorm had came through, the next morning the horses were covered in what looked like adobe armor after rolling in the mud hole in the middle of the corral after that rain. Her mother had helped her with that one they had taken the geldings over to the water faucet and washed them off with the hose. They then tied them up until they were completely dry so that they would not go roll in the mud again. After they had dried in the warm summer sun she had brushed them off even combing out their manes and tails. The two gelding looked like different horses after she had finished, it had taken her most of the afternoon but it was well worth it. Now every morning they were standing looking through the poles in the corral fence up toward the house waiting for her to come give them their feed and brushing.

With the little band of mares gone from the creek bottom she found herself with a lot of time on her hands, being anxious and out of boredom she had taken on the project of cleaning out the big barn. Starting with big loft she had swept and shoveled out all of the old straw, throwing the loose hay out the loft door down to the ground below where she would then put it in the wheel barrow and push it down to edge of the yard there she would scatter it out in the grass. Next she moved down into the big open main part of the bard like the loft it had accumulated several years of dust and debris. She swept and shoveled her piles into her wheelbarrow and took them out to the far edge of the yard and scattered it in the tall grass the fine dust making a big cloud as it settled into the grass.

The big main room of the barn took her several days to make it from one end to the other, with the exception of the new stack of the fresh hay she had swept every inch of the big room. After she had finished the barn she was ready to move into the tack room. This was going to be the most tedious part of the whole barn, there were so many things in this room. She decided that the only way that she could successfully clean it was to break it into smaller sections and clean them one at a time. The tack room alone took her a week, but it looked so much better and she felt so good about finishing it. The barn took her two weeks to clean, on the third week she helped her mother working in the yard and her garden. At the end of the third week she was pestering her mother about riding the geldings, finally her mother told her that there was still one week left and until that week was done the horses did not belong to them. They were only the care taker for the thirty days. It was obvious that neither gelding had been ridden for almost three years, even though they were both puppy-dog gentle and loved to be brushed and groomed everyday, they could be completely different once they were saddled, or even when they were being ridden.

Her mother continued telling her that for safety reasons in the event that the geldings were not claimed she had thought it to be a good idea to have someone else ride them for a few weeks just find out what kind of horses they were and how well broke they were. She had been talking to one of clients that lived across the valley, he was a good guy and she had been she had been told by several people that he was very handy with horses. His name was Vance, he started lots of colts every year and he was known for taking in older horses and giving them a good tune up. She had already talked to him twice and they had agreed that if the horses had not been claimed at the end of the thirty days and when they had made all of the necessary arrangements and had a clean Bill Of Sale they would be taking the horses directly to this man.

Samantha's hopes of riding the geldings were dashed for the time being, but she trusted her mother and she was sure that it would be well worth the wait. She thought to herself, by the time she could ride a horse she was going to have the whole place cleaned up there wouldn't be a rock that she hadn't turned over in the yard. Maybe that had been the plan all along. It was while having these thoughts that she was truck with an idea. She then ask her mother if she thought it would be ok if they could go watch while this fellow was working with the geldings. Her mother looked at her for a bit then she said that might be a good idea and that the next time she talked to the horse guy she would ask him just to make sure that it would be alright to do so.

Finally the thirty days were up, Samantha had, had a hard time sleeping the night before and when she came to breakfast she had prepared herself for the worst. Her mother had made biscuits and gravy one of her favorites, now she knew that there must be bad news and her mom was trying to make her feel better already. When she ask if they had heard anything about the geldings both her parents shook their heads and said no, no news yet. She ate the biscuits and gravy she had been more hungry than she had realized. With a good meal under her belt she felt some what better, but she was still anxious, she just wanted all of the waiting to be over. She had never even felt this way before even waiting for Christmas, maybe it was because she wanted something that she couldn't have or she had it, yet she didn't have it. After a while she decided that she should just quit thinking about it. Maybe today she after she finished her chores she would go back down to the creek bottom and see if maybe the little band of mares had returned. That would give her something to do away from the yard and she would be moving that always seemed to make waiting that much easier.

She walked back home slower than she normally did each step had a little bit of dread yet each step had a little bit of anxiety in it. She had spent most of her day just laying around in the tall grass in the shade of her favorite tree, in the grove of big cottonwoods. She didn't spend much time looking for the little band of mares she was sure that they had not returned, she had decided that she just needed to be away and by herself for a while. She had needed some time to reflect and to recharge. The big hatch of deer flies must have ran their course because she only swatted at a couple of them, hopefully they never returned either. As she came into view of the barn and the pens she could not help but to quicken her stride a little. As she walked by the barn the two geldings were still in the pen, so no one had came and taken them away today. When she walked up to the house her mom was setting in a patio chair at an outdoor table under a big cottonwood near the front door having a glass of ice tea. When she walked up she ask her mom if she had heard any news about the geldings she merely shook her head and said "nope not yet". "How was your day? Did you see any signs of the other horses?" Samantha only shook her head.

After they had sat at the patio for a while her mother got up and went inside and began making preparations to get supper started. Samantha went down to the barn and threw the two geldings some fresh hay then she hopped up on the big hay rack and sat between the two as they munched on the hay. They looked so much better now than they did the day they brought them in, their manes and tails were combed out and not tangle with sticks and old grass. She thought that they had even gained some weight since they had been here, after all the hay was of the very best quality. Over the last few weeks she had grown attached to the two geldings. She sat there for a while then she got down her dad would soon be home maybe he would have some news.

As she walked to the house she could see her dad's truck coming down the county road. She waited for him at the gate, as he got out he ask if there had been any news about the two geldings she only shook her head then they waked into the house together. The supper table was a quiet place that night they mostly ate in silence only talking when necessary. After the table was cleared and the dishes were done she went up to her room there she tried to read some in her book, but that was no use all she could think about was the two geldings that were down at the barn eating hay unconcerned. Finally she gave up went and took a shower and went to bed, to her surprise she was asleep when her head touched her pillow. That night her dreams were filled with her setting on the back of a running horse both of her hands holding handfuls of the long mane as the horse ran across high mountain slopes, the wind blowing in her hair and on her face. It was a feeling of freedom and the closest thing to flying she had ever experienced.

The next morning she woke up the dream still very clear in her head, she had to smile to herself as she ran it through her head once more. That was the most real and exciting dream she had ever had. When she got down to the breakfast table her dad had already gone, but her mom was there putting water in her plants that were hanging in various places around the kitchen and living room. They cleaned off the table and washed the dishes she went to the barn and threw the two geldings some fresh hay. She then went back to the house where they swept and mopped the kitchen as well as the living room then they dusted all of the furniture. It was close to lunch time by the time they had finished cleaning up the lower part of the house. Samantha kept thinking about the dream that she had, had she was sure that someday she would be able to ride just like she had in her dream, what a feeling it had been.

Finally late afternoon a pickup drove into the yard by the color and emblem on the door they knew it was the state brand inspector. Samantha's stomach kind of did a flip and landed on the bottom when she saw the brand inspector's truck drive up, it was show time, this was what they had been waiting for. The brand inspector got out and apologized for not getting there sooner but he had been called out on the far end of his district and had just gotten back. Larry could tell that the two gals were anxious to know about the two geldings so he got right to it. He said that they had, had only mild interest in the advertising a few phone calls asking about certain markings, but nobody had stepped up with any real intentions. He said if you guys still wanted them they are available. He said usually how it works was you had to pay for the last thirty days feed and care, but since you guys did all of that. How did a fifty dollar administration fee sound? The girl's knees were shaking she was so excited her mom went into the house and came back out with her checkbook and ask the inspector how she should fill it out? As she was making out the check the inspector was writing in a big book then he tore out two copies one pink and one blue the original stayed in the book when her mom handed him her check he gave her the two papers and said that they are all yours and he hoped that they made good horses for them. He thanked them then he got back in his pickup and drove away. Samantha and her mom just stood there looking at each other then Samantha let out a squeal and ran to the barn. Her mom walked over to the barn and looked at the two geldings through the gate hoping that they weren't just a couple of spoiled knot heads that somebody just turned loose in the mountains. Her intuition told her that they were both good guys and they would probably have a home here for the rest of their lives.

When her dad got home the excitedly told him the whole story about the brand inspector coming by and how they now owned the two geldings. That night at the supper table there was a lot of talking even some laughing as the meal was eaten. The long wait was over and the relief felt good to everyone. That night Samantha was almost to excited to even go to bed, but finally she did and she slept sound and happy. The next morning after breakfast her mom made the phone call to the man named Vance across the valley that had agreed to ride the two geldings for a while, at least until they knew for sure how well they were broke and how they behaved when ridden. She ask him about them coming over to watch and if that would be alright. He replied to her that he didn't mind that at all, but just to be on the safe side they should wait for a few days until he had evaluated the two geldings. Sometimes when horses hadn't been saddled or ridden for a long period of time they could react in a very loud and violent manner before settling back into their old training. If they did show signs of being spoiled or ill mannered their behavior could be scary for a young girl that had never been around that kind of a thing before. "We don't want to frighten her away before she ever gets started" Her mother agreed that was probably the best they could come a few days later. She told him that they could bring the two geldings over on the weekend and so it was set up the count down on another game of wait and see had begun.

First thing Saturday morning right after breakfast her dad went out and hooked his truck up to the goose neck trailer, it had been setting there when they came to the place. After hooking up the trailer her dad pulled it to the shop where he checked the air in all of the tires, they looked to be in good condition. He hoped that they were good enough to make the short trip over the place were they were taking the two geldings. Samantha and her mom went to the barn and caught the two gelding and led them out while her dad was checking out the trailer. He drove to the barn and parked, when they opened the back gate and lead the geldings up they both stepped right in with no hesitations, after they tied them towards the front they all climbed into the pickup and began the drive to the horse trainers place. It was not that far it took them less than an hour to drive across to the opposite side of the valley it was near a small range of very rugged mountains that ran parallel to the valley. The horseman's place was at the mouth of a jagged canyon that came down out of these rugged little mountains, there was a big cottonwood tree on either side of his house and his barn was more of a lean to. He had two round pens one much larger than the other connecting in the middle, a roping arena that also connected to the larger round pen and several pens of different sizes it was a nice place in a neat location.

They stopped in front of the round pen where the man was just finishing up with a young horse, he tied the horse to a good spot in the corral then he came out and introduced himself. After all of the formalities They untied the two geldings and walked to the back of the goose neck trailer, opening the gate her mom stepped into the trailer and brought out the bay gelding handed him to Samantha then brought out the sorrel gelding. Both geldings stood with their ears forward and heads high taking in all of the new surroundings Vance motioned them to one of the larger pens and said they would be fine there. He had already filled the big tire feeder with some fresh hay. The geldings went straight to it and began to eat the hay, then Vance said that he would leave them there for the rest of the day and let them get familiar with their new place and then tomorrow he would introduce himself to them. The girls parents and the horseman visited at the pen for a while then they got back in the pickup and made the return trip back home. Samantha was hopeful that she could come back soon.

The little family spent the rest of the weekend together, even going into town and having dinner at the cafe. It was only the second time since they had moved there that girl had eaten at the cafe it was good and on the way back home they stopped and got ice cream. It was a grand night out for Samantha. With the two geldings away the place seemed empty she had not realized how much time she had spent with the two geldings until they weren't there. She did not know what she was going to do until they were back either. It was going to be another game of wait, it sure seemed like she had done a lot of that lately. Maybe now was the time that she could read one of the books that she had gotten last spring before school had let out. She was sure that the only reason to go to the creek bottom was sit under her tree there in the grove of the big cottonwoods, for the little band of mares to be there she had given up on that idea. They were gone and she had no idea in what direction.

Thursday night after they had cleared the table and done the dishes the phone rang it was the horseman calling. After about a twenty minute conversation her mom hung up the phone and came back into the living room. She sat back down on the couch all eyes were on her then she smiled and said that Vance had invited them to come out Saturday afternoon and he would ride the two geldings for them. He would explain everything that he had learned about the two and what his evaluation was thus far. He had been very impressed with both of the two geldings.

Saturday had finally gotten there after having an early lunch they had climbed into her dads pickup and they were on their way to see the two geldings. Even though it was less than an hour away it seemed to take forever to get to the horseman's place. When they drove in the first thing they saw were the two gelding standing tied to a hitching rail their heads down one hip cocked dozing in the sun. The geldings did raise their heads when the pickup came to a stop and Samantha and her parents got out. Samantha went straight to the two geldings petting and rubbing their heads, they stood there taking it all in enjoying the girl rubbing on their heads. Vance came out from somewhere and shook hands with her mom and dad before walking over to the hitching rack. He said that he wanted them to see everything starting with being saddled. He lead the sorrel gelding over to the little saddle shed there he quickly saddle the sorrel gelding, the gelding stood still as a statue hardly even moving his ears. He returned the sorrel to the hitching rail then he took the bay gelding to the shed taking out another saddle he saddle the bay gelding and his reaction was very much the same as the sorrel gelding's had been. Grabbing two bridles from a peg just inside the door of the little saddle shed he led the bay gelding to the bigger round pen, there he hung one bridle on a peg near the gate and the other he put on the bay gelding, opened the gate and led the gelding into the pen.

Once inside he checked his cinch and took it up several holes, he began by saying that as best he could tell by looking at their teeth they were both around ten years old. Speaking of their teeth he said that it would probably be a good idea to take both of the gelding to a vet and get their teeth floated, there was no telling what kind of condition they might be in. He then went on to say that he was pretty sure that both geldings had been flunk-outs, by that he meant that they had been started and then professionally trained for several months before they failed to make the cut. They had probably been trained and taken as far as they could go before it was determined that they could not get any better and they would never be the big champion that the owners were looking for. It was numbers game and they fell short, that was not to say that they weren't still great horses it just meant they would never be show horses at the high levels. The owners then cut their losses and go back and look for their next champion. These two had probably made it to the second or third cut, they had to of gotten that far for them to be as broke as they were.

He then stepped on the bay gelding, the gelding stood calmly waiting for instructions from the horseman. Vance lifted the reins a gave a little squeeze with his feet and the gelding moved off smooth and willingly. Then Vance put the gelding through several small maneuvers letting him get warmed up before asking him to do anything real demanding, he loped the bay gelding in circles both ways the gelding effortlessly picking up his leads going both ways. After he was warmed up good the horseman ever so slightly picked up his hand and relaxed his legs and whispered the word whoa and the gelding melted underneath him his head dropping and his hind feet sliding up under him coming to a complete stop. Samantha heard her mom say in a low voice "wow" Samantha was smiling the whole time watching the bay gelding being rode. Vance then rode the gelding into a small circle making it smaller and smaller until he was spinning like a top he did this both ways then he ask the gelding to backup the horse dropped his head and went backwards as well as he went forwards. He told them he does it all. The only thing he hadn't done was tried them on cattle if he wanted to leave them for one more week he would take them to a friends place and see how they did there. They were welcome to come along if they wanted to.

He then stepped down from the bay took the bridle off and put the halter back on led him out the gate to the tie rack and exchanged him for the sorrel. He led the sorrel gelding into the big pen and did the same thing that he had done with the bay gelding. When he had finished he said that the sorrel was much more responsive and was a lot quicker than the bay gelding was there for he didn't think that he would be a good choice for a beginning rider just starting out. He then said that if one of them wanted to get on the bay gelding he would ride along with them until they felt comfortable and them see how it was for themselves. Her mom went over and untied the bay gelding and led him back to the big pen took the bridle from the peg and put it on she then adjusted the stirrups to as close as she could calculate that they should be then she stepped on. Samantha had never seen her mother ride a horse before and she was impressed her mother rode very well and she handled the bay gelding very much the same as Vance had. When she had ridden the bay for a while they switched horses and she rode the sorrel gelding and Vance rode the bay. When they had finished they led the two geldings to the little saddle shed and unsaddled them and turned them loose in their pen. Before they left they agreed to go with Vance to see how the geldings did on cattle.

As they made the drive back home her mom said that she was relieved to find out that the two geldings were both good guys, the fact that they were as outstanding as they were was a pure blessing, it could have gone the other way just as easily. They could have both been someone's back yard pet that had been spoiled rotten and sap heads to ride. She was excited and really looking forward to bringing the two geldings home.

They would bring them home right after they saw how they worked the cattle and they would start riding the geldings themselves. Samantha liked the idea of that, she was ready to start riding and stop walking.

They took the goose neck trailer with them when they went to meet the horseman at the place with the cattle, today would be the last day that the two geldings would be away from them. Samantha was about as excited as she as she could remember ever being, she wanted to see the horses work, but she really wanted to bring them home so she could ride. The pulled into the place where they were meeting the horseman, all it was was some pens and a roping arena. The pens at the end of the of the arena were full of cattle they presumed that would be some of the ones that they would be working. Right behind them Vance drove in with the two geldings in his trailer and he parked beside them. He got out said "hello" and unloaded the geldings they were both already saddled, he ask her mother if she wanted to ride the bay gelding as he put a bridle on the sorrel gelding. She agreed and he handed her a bridle, she put it on the bay gelding then they led the two geldings into the arena checked the cinches and stepped on, they began riding the geldings around putting them through some manuevores getting them warmed up and ready to work the cattle. After about a half an hour of loping in circles and practicing some stops and turn a rounds the geldings were ready to work the cattle. It was about that time that two other people a man and his wife rode up to the arena and introduced themselves, his name was Fred and her name was Kathy they were the people that owned the arena and the cattle and they were going help with the works today.

Fred went into one the pens and brought out about ten head of the cattle, he brought them up the alley and out into the arena. The cattle kind of bucked and played when they got out in the soft sand and the openness of the arena, being out of the pen and out into the bigger area made them feel fresh. As they brought the cattle back to the end of the arena the man began riding in around and through the cattle getting them to settle so that they would stay in place when they were being worked. After several minutes he rode out and motioned to Vance that they were ready. Her mother moved up the side of the small herd and the Kathy went to the other side and Fred stayed out in front of the herd as Vance slowly rode into the herd. He held the reins a little high in his left hand, as he rode around in the herd he finally settled which cow that he wanted to cut out. When he got the cow singled out and all of the other cattle had moved back into the herd he dropped his hand down on the sorrel gelding neck and the gelding began working he cow on his own. He mirrored every move that cow made when the cow tried to get back in the herd the sorrel gelding was poised and in it's way, when the cow tried to leave the Fred who was setting out in front would turn it back into the sorrel that would in turn block it from going to the herd. Finally the cow just gave up, when it did so Vance put his free hand on the gelding's neck and picked up the reins again turned the gelding back into the herd were they cut out another cow.

Vance cut out two more cows and worked them before riding over to her mom and giving her the sorrel and he got on the bay gelding. He rode the bay gelding into the herd and cut out three cows on him, he did really well but not near as good as the sorrel gelding had done. When the had finished they put the cattle back in to the pen and then the rode out of the arena and over to where the trailers were parked. They unsaddled the two geldings putting the saddles in Vance's trailer, they put their halters on the geldings and loaded them into their goose neck trailer. Her mom then took out her checkbook and wrote the horseman a check for the work that he had done with the two geldings. They all stood around talking for a while before shaking hands and then they were on their way home, the long wait was finally over.

When they got back home they unloaded the geldings and put them back in their corral and made sure that the big hay rack had plenty of fresh hay in it. Since it was past lunch time they went up to the house and they all had a sandwich as they were eating her dad told them that he needed to go check on a load of material that was supposed to be delivered that afternoon so he would be home later in the afternoon. That left her and her mom to make a plan for them and the two geldings. After her dad left her and her mom went down to the barn, they went into the tack room. Here her mom started taking the tarps that covered the saddles off until she found what she was looking for, she had uncovered a well worn saddle that was flower tooled, Samantha was sure that it had been a real work of art when it was new. Her mom wiped the dust off and told her "a saddle maker from Sheridan Wy. By the name of Don Butler had made it for her uncle years ago" it had been his favorite saddle. She remembered riding it a couple of times when she was helping her uncle, the seat fit like a glove and she always liked the saddle, it was going to be her saddle now. After she had dusted the saddle off she looked under a couple more of the tarps til she found what she was looking for. It was a smaller saddle, it was not near as wore as the other one but it had seen considerable use. She looked at the girl and said "this can be your saddle it was the one I use to ride when I was your age", the girls heart shipped a beat as she said that. She had not even thought about a saddle she just wanted to ride the horses, then she thought of the dream she had all she was holding was two handfuls of mane, this was a much better deal. Her mother went to the rack where all of the saddle pads and blankets were hanging there she picked out two sets of the newer looking ones and set them on top of the two saddles. After she had checked the ladigos, half-breeds, and cinches she moved over to the wall that was covered with bridles and hackamores she looked through them until she found two that were close to the ones that Vance had been using. She took these down and moved them to the pegs that were above both of the saddles there she hung them so that they would be there when they were ready to use them. Over in one corner on a set of shelves were several pairs of riding boots some of them had been hers as she was growing up, some she had outgrown and a couple pair that she had worn the last summer she had been here with her uncle. She looked them over then she handed the girl a pair and told her to try them on, she then took down a pair of newer larger ones and tried them on herself. To her surprise they still fit and the boots she had given to the girl were a little bit big but they were ok maybe she could wear two pair of socks. She walked around the tack room looking at everything again for the very first time.

The tack room was like going back in time and it brought back a lot of fond memories there had been a lot good days that had started right here in this tack room and there had been a lot of long hard days that had ended here as well. The smell of the leather and the sweat covered saddle pads, the dust it all came together and made it's own smell that was unique to that tack room. All tack rooms had their own particular smell. She took the two halters that were hanging from the peg by the door and she handed one to the girl as she walked past and out into the corral where the two gelding were standing head to tail. She caught the sorrel gelding and Samantha caught the bay gelding. They led them back into the barn to two of the tie rings that were attached to the wall, they brushed them off and then her mom walked her through all of the steps of getting one saddled. When it came time for the her to put the saddle on even though it was smaller it still felt heavy to her. Her mom walked down to end of the barn where she picked up a square box that looked like a two step stairs case, she brought it over and set it next to the bay gelding he didn't seem to mind then she told her this was what she use to use, you can just walk up on it and put your saddle on.

Samantha had to saddle and unsaddle the bay gelding several times until her mom felt that she had a good idea about everything, then they took the two gelding out into the bright sun light and into the big pen. Once outside Samantha suddenly became aware of the fact that she was about ride her first horse, her knees started to tremble with excitement that she was suddenly over whelmed with. He mother noticed the uncertainty in the girls face and reassured her that it was going to be alright. After she tied the sorrel gelding under the lean to she came back and put a bridle on the bay she left the halter on just in case she had to step in and help out somewhere along the way. She then helped the girl climb on the bay gelding he stood still as a rock and as patient as a saint as the girl awkwardly climbed on. The big grin that was on the girls face told her all that she needed to know. After they got the girls stirrups adjusted to the right length she handed the girl the reins and she took the lead rope and led the bay gelding around the corral a few times letting the girl get use to the feel of how the horse was moving and how she should be setting in the saddle. There was a lot going on and the girl was like a sponge she was soaking up all of it.

Her mom had gotten on the sorrel gelding and was riding him around with her showing her how and what to do then having her do the same thing. At first it was confusing and strange the way everything felt, but as she became more comfortable with being on the back of a horse the more easier things became. As she showed the girl the basic skills of riding and handling a horse her mind drifted back to when she first started coming out to spend the summers with her uncle. He had taught so much and now she was able to share those same lessons with her own daughter it was bitter sweet as she thought back on how much she had learned from her uncle not just about horses but about life. He had been so patient with her, she was now following his lead on the same subject. They spent most of the afternoon work on the most basic things she wanted to be sure that the girl was comfortable and confident and that she had a good foundation from which to work from. At first nothing made much sense but as she continued working on foot, leg and hand position it slowly came together for her. The bay gelding handled everything like a champ he never got cranky with the girl no matter how awkward or in his way she was he just took it all in stride, he was very forgiving to the girl. When her mom could tell that she had probably had all that she could possibly absorb she suggested that she just ride around the pen and work on getting the feel of being horseback.

After they had unsaddled and fed the two gelding they went up to the house where they sat in the shade at the patio table and drank some cool water, it had been a good day and the afternoon was one of the best ever. It was sure to be one that neither of them would forget anytime soon. When her mother ask Samantha how she felt she said that there were some muscles in her legs that were sore that she had never felt before. He mom just laughed and said that is what everyone says after their very first time riding.

After a few days of working on basics inside the corral her mom decided that they needed to go for a ride outside and let their minds decompress. They rode out of the yard heading in the direction of the creek bottom they took the trail leading that way the two geldings eager to be outside stepped out at a good walk they were at the rim over looking the creek bottom here they stopped. They looked up and down the creek then they went down the trail into the bottom riding over to the grove big cottonwood trees. Next they rode over to the little side canyon were they had last seen the little band of mares, they rode all the way up past the narrow bend and out into the big opening with the rock rims. The two gelding were looking around as well, looking for the little band of mares that hey had spent the last couple of years with. The only horse tracks that were there were the ones that were coming out behind them.

Almost everyday they would spend part of it horseback if not out finding new places and exploring the country side they would work on horsemanship skills in the coral at the barn. Samantha was learning fast it seemed like she just couldn't get enough of the riding thing, she was learning a lot from her mom and the bay gelding was teaching her a lot as well. By the time school started the girl had become confident and comfortable being horseback she could walk and trot and lope circles, she could pick up a soft feel and she could side pass the bay gelding. She dreaded having to go back to school this had been one of the best summer she had ever had.

Almost every afternoon when she got off of the school bus she would look over at the barn to see if her mom had the horses saddled, if they were she would run to the house change from her school clothes into her riding clothes grab a snack on the way out then head straight to the barn. There her mom would be waiting with the horses saddled bridled and ready to go. They rode many miles that fall they rode as many afternoons that they could even if the weather got a little cool or blustery they would just bundle up and go. They even rode one Saturday when it was snowing straight down The quiet stillness of the day left them both in awe, it had been one of the best rides that they had ever been on.

CHAPTER
Twenty

The fall works was well under way they had most all of the cattle pushed down from the very high pastures. The works had gone off as usual except that they had an unusually heavy snow up in the higher country, the snow level had stayed about half way up, down below they had gotten rain not a lot but it had made the work wet and sloppy for the men as they worked the cattle in the pens. In the higher meadow it had dumped over a foot of the white stuff covering up all of the available grass. They were working at the big pens at the head quarters, they were in the process of weaning the last set of calves, the alley was full and there were two big pens left to run through. That was when everyone stopped what they were doing and they all looked up and saw all of the horses coming off of the long slope to the barn at a dead run. At first someone said there must be a mountain lion after them, nobody commented they just continued to watch. Keith who was doing the sorting looked at the bunch of horses and he knew as soon as he saw the bay roan and the blue roan what was going on, he sat there on his horse watching as the horses came running through the big double gate and into the big pole lot where they usually penned the cattle when they brought them in from that side. They ran into the lot and began milling and squealing and kicking the air was damp and chilly so they were full of themselves. Their heads were up their tails sticking straight out and they were dancing around that in that big strided trot everyone called "the wild mare trot" with good reason they were acting like wild mares.

Keith told his guys to close all of their gates and he went out and loped to upper side of the big pole lot and closed the two gates. He then had one of his guys open the gate and let the horses down into the big corral by the barn, he waited until the gates were set then he pushed the stirred up bunch of horses into the big pen they were still squealing, kicking and biting at each other. He motioned for one his guys to come over and watch the gate while he sorted this stuff out, he then told another one of the guys to open another gate that went into another joining corral. He told them that he wanted to let all of their saddle horse back out, but he wanted to keep the three older mares and the two roan mares in the pens and they could go into the other pen if it happened to work out that way. He then told one of his guys to start bringing the horses out he would set in the gate. The horses had settled down quite a bit there was just a squeal and a kick once in a while. The horses knew the routine and they began going out the gate as the rider sorted them out. They had all gone out except for two of the geldings and they had attached them to the mares they were running up and down acting like they to were some kind of wild things. He closed the gate and then they ushered mares and two geldings into the adjoining corral. When they rode into the corral to get the geldings out, that was when the two roan mares realized that they were in a trap and the panic set in. Living their entire lives running loose on the mountains they had never felt the confinement of a corral. The bay roan mare ran at the high pole fence and tried to jump but she only slid along it and bounced off, a lesson learned. The blue roan mare ran by one men kicked at his horse and then ran almost up to the pole fence sliding in the mud crashing head long into the fence falling back over on her side.

She jumped up unhurt and ran back to the safety of the bunch the two gelding that had been so eager to be with them decided that the mares were to wild for them and they trotted to the gate the man setting in the gate moved his horse out of the way and let them pass. One of the men in the corral looking at the three older mares made the comment that all three of those mares had the ranch brand on them. Why had he never seen them before? Where had they been running at?

After the break form the sorting alley and all of the excitement of the mixed up horses they took a quick break had a cup of coffee and some snacks then back into the sorting pens they went the loud den of the bawling cattle was all any one could hear. They sorted the cattle for another two hours or more before they finished the last bunch the guys in the back that had been pushing the cattle up had tied up their horses and had the old flatbed truck loaded with hay. They were in one of the big water lots driving around in circles scattering out the hay so they could put the fresh weaned calves in the pen where they would stay until they had quit their bawling. The cows they would only open the gate, most of them would leave maybe go get a drink of water maybe eat some grass before they remembered that they had left there calves back at the pens, then here they would come back bawling looking for their calf. This usually went on for around three days once in a while it took longer. The calves would eat some of the hay at first but mostly walk and ball and after about three days they would be eating the hay and not thinking to much about mama any longer. They would pen all of the cows again tomorrow and work them down the chute vaccinating checking to see how many were with calf and how many would wind up in the cull pen. This process usually took a lot of the bawl out of the cows and most of them would usually have gone back to their home range by the third day.

The day had been heavy overcast all day so it was almost dark by the time they had finished taking care of the cattle, they had brought the horses back in before they turned them out and caught fresh horses for the next day. They turned their tired horses loose and fed them good then they feed their fresh horse as well as the five mares in the next corral. The fact that the three older mares had the ranch brand on them had stirred up the curiosity in the men. They stood looking through the poles at the mares as they ate the fresh hay the two roan mares standing off to the side not trusting anything right now. Keith told the men a quick story about the three older mares and how the roan mares came to be, he was careful to mention that they were only two and three years old when they left and they had been living wild in the mountains ever since. Apparently this had been the first time for the two roan mares to ever even be in a corral and this was probably the first time for the older mares since they left this corral all those years ago. As they were looking at the mares one of the Billy noticed the scars that ran the length of the bay mare's neck, there was two long scars on the left side of her neck that extended down to her shoulder and three long ones on her right side. Looking closer they saw some scars on her chest as well, they all agreed that she did not get them from going through a fence. Cole said "Mountain lion".

It was getting dark so the men moved off in their own direction for the night Keith went up to his house thinking how things had worked out. He had been thinking about making an attempt at bringing the little band of horses into the pens, he knew that it could be a real chore and require some hard and dangerous riding. He had thought about this a lot and had been thinking after all of the cow work was done if the little band was still hanging around the Big Meadow maybe he would take a couple of the better hands up there and see if they could bring them down. It was funny how these things had a way of sorting them selves out the mares had probably been pushed out of the Big Meadow by that last big storm up there and they had drifted right into the horses and they pretty much penned them selves. He admitted to himself that he was relieved and excited when he saw those mares with all of the saddle horses coming into the corral on their own. That was a stroke of good luck.

It had been close to a month since the day that the five mares had come in with the saddle horses, he had decided to keep them in the pen hoping that the two roan mares would settle down and maybe even get gentle. Everyday at one of the men would go into the pen either on foot or horseback and move in, out and around the mares the three older mares settled down right away, but it took a while for the two roan mares to catch on to the idea. Good feed and an empty belly are good motivators eventually the two roan mares would stand still and let them put out their hay, once in a while one of them would even come up and start eating while who ever had fed was still standing there. They would come around in time they all agreed on that. They had sort of became the group project. Keith wasn't looking forward to the end of the cow work, everyone would go back to their respectful places and start getting things ready for winter, Keith would once again have the whole place to himself. He kind of liked having all the other men around for the cow work, but he did like it when it was just himself around.

They were down to the last of the work which was to gather and take all of the weaned calves to the lower pastures where they would spend the winter before being moved up to the Big Meadow in the high country for the summer. They had sorted all of the steers from the heifers and they had them in separate meadows along the creek. After the one big storm that mostly stayed up on the mountain the weather had straightened out they had experienced pleasant weather for the rest of the works. The calves had all weaned good and they hadn't had any sickness in them thus far, they were about past the breaking period for that and things were looking good in that area. They had even been able to make two trips back up into the higher country both times bringing down cattle that had been missed, the second time they picked up the rest of the cattle and to everyone's relief that satisfied the count. Things were winding down fast all of the cows were happy and out on their winter range, the nice weather was still hanging in there, everyone was looking forward to going back home and being done with all of the cow work.

They were all saddled up the plan for the day was to make one last ride through all of the weaned calves and make sure everything was in good shape before they all left for their winter homes. They were standing around talking, and waiting for the Keith to come to the barn when he came walking into the corral, he spoke to everyone, grabbed his halter and walked out into the big pen and caught his horse, led him back to the barn and saddled him. Everyone was standing around watching him knowing they were about hear some kind of late breaking news and that they probably would not be going home the following day. When he finished saddling his horse he told them that he had been on the phone with Brad Smith, the fellow that had bought the calves last year and he wanted to buy them again this year. Keith had told him that he wasn't interested when this cow buyer added a new twist to the deal. Brad wanted to take them to some corn stalks at farm that he had leased for the winter, this farm was only about two hundred miles from the ranch. He then wanted to send them back and have them summer the yearlings in the high country. After he had ran all of the numbers and with the market was up right now and with the amount that Brad was willing to pay for the grass and the care for the summer. "That would mean that a couple of you guys would have jobs for the summer". To make it even better it would eliminate most of the risk on his part, it was a to good of a deal to pass on. There was just one catch that is when everyone snickered saying they "knew it", but he said it's not that bad they just want to take delivery in three days." We can do it we will just have to ride a little harder" with that everyone had a little laughed.

By the time they had the last bunch of weaned calves pushed up into the shipping trap and ready for shipping the following day the wind had begun to pick up and the dark clouds were rolling over the mountains. There was a change in the weather coming and probably wasn't one for the better. By the time they closed the gate and rode to the barn the temperature had dropped considerably. They unsaddled their tired horses and caught some fresh ones for the next day, they filled the big hay rack under the lean to with fresh hay put some hay out to the five mares in the next pens then they called it a day.

The wind blew all night and the next morning when they were catching horse there a few drops of rain starting to fall, with the little bit of rain the wind stopped. After they caught all of their horse they moved the little band of mares into the big pen with the lean to were they had been keeping their horses. They would need to fill the corral that the little band of mares had been in with weaned calves. The men stepped on their horses and went to the shipping traps and began bringing up the calves, they started with the steer calves first. By the time they had the last calf in the corral and the gate closed a pickup truck drove up to the pens and two men got out Larry the brand inspector was already there setting in his pickup. Down the road a ways were a line of semi trucks their lights still on waiting for the word to come up to the pens and begin filling heir big trailers with the weaned calves. Keith told two of the men Cole and Billy to come with him and for rest to start bringing in the heifer calves. They pushed the steer calves into the pen where the little band of mares had been and began filling the alley Keith then rode over to the scale house got down tied up his horse and went inside joining the two men that had driven up in truck. They shook hands then he balanced the scale and waved to Cole and Billy who were waiting horseback in the ally ready to bring cattle down the ally and onto the scales.

The two men horse back brought the drafts of cattle on to the scales were they were weighed and Larry would count them out the other side as they went off of the scales. His job was get a good head count and verify that the brands were all correct and there not be any neighbors or stray cattle in the bunch. They were getting down to the end of the steer calves when the men that had been sent back to bring in the heifer calves came into view, the heifers were moving briskly with cooler weather. As the last draft of steer calves were counted off of the scales Cole and Billy who had been bringing them across the scales set the gates and went out to help the men bringing in the heifer calves. Together they all got the heifers penned and began the weighing process again, this time it was the heifers. After the heifers were penned the man that had came with Brad got in the pickup truck drove down and old the truckers that they could come up and start loading their trucks. Keith then split his crew send Cole and Billy to start the process of loading the steer calves and other three to stay back and start bringing the heifers to the scale so they to could be weighed. The whole thing resembled a well orchestrated military maneuver every one hustling and working together.

The first truck drove up and backed up to the load out at the end of the ally, the driver got out told Cole how he wanted the cattle brought to him and then he and Billy began bringing the steers up the ally to load the trucks, while the rest were weighing the heifers. The rain began to fall more steadily as the cattle work continued and by the time the last steers were loaded and the heifers were weighed the rain was coming down soaking everything. When they began loading the heifers the rain was coming down hard and there was beginning to be a few flakes of snow mixed in. By the time that they had loaded the last truck the rain had turned to snow the big flakes sticking to the backs of the heifers turning them white. The snow sticking to everything steam coming from the horses as they carried the men up and down the ally's bringing the cattle to the trucks to be loaded. Finally the last truck was loaded and his gate was dropped, big flakes of snow still coming down. The last truck had pulled away and Keith and Brad along with Tom the man that had came with Brad went back to the scale house. Larry had filled out all of his paperwork and had given Brad his copy and had made sure that the truck drivers all had their hauling papers then he was on his way. While they had been weighing the cattle they had built a fire in the little wood stove that was inside the scale house and the little scale house was warm when they stepped back into it.

Brad and Keith did all of the math and paper work that is involved in the process of selling cattle and Brad had filled out an invoice and then he wrote Keith a check for the price that they had agreed on. They were standing in the warm little scale house looking out the window across the big pen at the snow coming down. The three older mares were standing head to tail under the lean to next to the big hay rack full of fresh hay. For the most part they had remained dry in spite of the heavy rain and snow that had been falling all morning, the two younger roan mares were standing on the back side of the corral, the snow covering their backs. As the two men were looking across at the three mares standing under the lean to the Brad ask Keith "what's the story on that little bunch?" pointing his chin toward the mares under the lean to. After a long and thoughtful pause Keith said softly "I wish I knew".